"Let me out. This

The words came out o
would have been embarrassing in s
in a state of shock. "Where exactly are we going.

He made one more turn, braked and then backed
into a parking space outside a six-story, terraced
Georgian house. He switched off the engine and,
slinging his arm over the steering wheel, angled his
body toward her. "We're here. The appointment's
not for another—" he glanced at his watch "—ten
minutes," he announced, as if that explained
everything.

She peered past him and read the street sign on
the corner. "What are we doing on Harley Street?"

The house he'd stopped in front of had an ornate
brass plaque listing two doctors' names. That made
sense. Harley Street was the domain of London's
most exclusive private medical practitioners. But
nothing else did. Why had he brought her here?

He took his sunglasses off, flung them in the back
seat. "Answer me one question," he said, his voice
tight with annoyance. "Were you ever going to tell
me about it?"

"Tell you about what?" Why was he looking at her
as if she'd tried to steal the crown jewels and he'd
caught her red-handed?

His gaze wandered down to her abdomen. She
folded her arms, feeling oddly defensive. "About
my baby, of course. What else?"

ONE NIGHT BABY

When passion leads to pregnancy!

All-consuming attraction...spine-tingling kisses...unstoppable desire.

With tall, handsome, sexy, gorgeous men like these, it's easy to get carried away with the passion of the moment—and end up unexpectedly, accidentally, shockingly PREGNANT!

And whether she's his one-night lover, temporary love slave at work or permanent mistress, family life is not in his plan—well, not yet, anyway! The sparks will fly, the passion will ignite and their whole worlds will be turned upside down—and that's before the little bundle of joy has even arrived!

Don't miss any books in this exciting new miniseries from Harlequin Presents!

Heidi Rice

PLEASURE, PREGNANCY AND A PROPOSITION

ONE NIGHT BABY

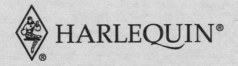

HARLEQUIN®

TORONTO • NEW YORK • LONDON
AMSTERDAM • PARIS • SYDNEY • HAMBURG
STOCKHOLM • ATHENS • TOKYO • MILAN • MADRID
PRAGUE • WARSAW • BUDAPEST • AUCKLAND

Recycling programs
for this product may
not exist in your area.

ISBN-13: 978-0-373-12809-9
ISBN-10:   0-373-12809-6

PLEASURE, PREGNANCY AND A PROPOSITION

First North American Publication 2009.

www.eHarlequin.com

Printed in U.S.A.

All about the author...
Heidi Rice

HEIDI RICE was born and bred—and still lives—in London, England. She has two boys who love to bicker, a wonderful husband who, luckily for everyone, has loads of patience, and a supportive and ever-growing British/French/Irish/American family.

As much as Heidi adores "the Big Smoke," she also loves America, and every two years or so she and her best friend leave hubby and kids behind and *Thelma and Louise* it across the States for a couple of weeks (although they always leave out the driving-off-a-cliff bit).

She's been a film buff since her early teens, and a romance junkie for almost as long. She indulged her first love by being a film reviewer for ten years. Then, two years ago, she decided to spice up her life by writing romance. Discovering the fantastic sisterhood of romance writers (both published and unpublished) in Britain and America made it a wild and wonderful journey to her first Harlequin novel, and she's looking forward to many more to come.

To my dad, Peter Rice, who I wish I could talk to just one more time.

And to Julia, Kieran and Nemone, because talking to you guys is the next best thing.

CHAPTER ONE

'QUICK, Lou, major hottie alert. Twelve o'clock.'

Louisa DiMarco's fingers paused on the keyboard of her computer at the urgent whisper from her editorial assistant, Tracy. 'I'm on deadline here, Trace,' she muttered. 'And I happen to take my work seriously.'

Louisa was a professional. One of *Blush* magazine's most popular and well-respected feature writers. Just because this article about the pros and cons of breast enlargement was giving her a headache—what were the pros anyway?—she would not be distracted from it because Tracy had spotted some good-looking guy in the office.

'We're talking scorching,' Tracy crooned. 'You will not want to miss this guy.'

Louisa kept her head down and carried on typing. For about two seconds.

'For goodness' sake!' She clicked on her screen to save. 'All right, one quick peek. But this had better be good.' Surely even a dedicated features writer like herself was entitled to some recreational pursuits on the hottest, stuffiest, most boring Friday afternoon in the history of the world ever?

Louisa peered round her computer to get a better view

of the vast open-plan office, not expecting to be impressed. Tracy's taste in men generally stank. Still, even Tracy's idea of what constituted a hottie couldn't make Louisa feel as queasy as the pictures she'd been looking at all afternoon. 'Where is Adonis, then?' she asked.

'Over there.' Tracy pointed to the far end of the office. 'The bloke with Piers,' she said, her voice hushed in reverence. 'Isn't he magnificent?'

Louisa sent her assistant a quick grin. Good to know she wasn't the only stir-crazy female on the premises. She looked past the desks of journalists typing like crazy on the last Friday before press day, and spied two men with their backs to the room by the receptionist's desk.

Louisa blinked. Tracy hadn't just surprised her. She'd astonished her. Louisa was the office's acknowledged hottie connoisseur and even she couldn't fault the guy. Not from this angle anyway. Tall, dark and broad shouldered, with an expertly tailored navy-blue designer suit, Adonis was making their managing editor, Piers Parker, who was at least five foot ten, look like a midget.

'What do you think?' Tracy said impatiently.

Louisa tilted her head to one side to get a better look. Even from fifty feet away the man deserved an appreciative purr. 'Well, he certainly qualifies from the rear,' she purred. 'But I think we'd need to see his face to make a final appraisal. As you know, no one enters the DiMarco Hottie Hall of Fame until they've passed the face test.'

Standing stiffly with his legs braced apart, Adonis chose that moment to thrust one fist into his trouser pocket. His body language radiated controlled irritation. Louisa didn't care. The movement had made his jacket rise up over his butt, improving the view even more. Now, if he would just turn around and come a bit closer…

Something teased the edges of Louisa's memory as she pressed her pen against her bottom lip and waited. She ignored it. This was definitely an improvement on silicone implants.

The clatter of computer keyboards and the buzz of conversation slowly tapered off as every woman in the place became aware of the designer-suited stranger in their midst. Louisa could almost hear a collective oestrogen-loaded sigh over the hum of expectation.

'Maybe he's the new assistant editor?' Tracy said hopefully.

'I doubt it. That suit's new season Armani, and Piers is practically genuflecting—which means Adonis is either on the board of directors or he's an Arsenal player,' Louisa whispered back.

Although she wouldn't be surprised if he *was* a sportsman, with that lean, athletic build, Louisa couldn't imagine a professional footballer looking so debonair.

Louisa fluffed her hair instinctively. Goodness, she was actually holding her breath. It had been so long since she'd had the urge to flirt she almost didn't recognise the feeling. How long had it been since she'd felt excited in the presence of a good-looking man?

The errant thought had an image forming that she instantly repressed. Do not go there. Her radar had been spectacularly off that day, but it had been over three months ago. Twelve weeks, four days and—she did a quick calculation—sixteen hours, to be exact. Luke Devereaux, the handsome, charming Lord of Berwick and bona fide snake in the grass, no longer had the power to upset her. But the prickle of memory developed into a nasty little thorn, scratching at her consciousness.

Louisa's brow furrowed as Piers turned to point straight

at her. How odd. Adonis followed in slow motion, but then a pair of piercing and painfully familiar grey eyes fixed on her face, and the little thorn became a jagged blade slicing through the sensual mist.

Louisa's fingers went numb, her heart thudded like a sledgehammer, all her blood rocketed into her cheeks, and the hairs on the back of her neck felt as if a greedy fist had wrenched them out at the roots. And then heat blazed through her body as the memory she'd been repressing for the last three months hit her like a red-hot slap—strong fingers stroking her, insistent lips fastened on the pulse-point in her neck, and wave upon glorious wave of orgasm rocketing up from her core.

A tangle of nerves, fury and nausea snaked into a vicious knot in the pit of her stomach.

What was *he* doing here?

That was no Adonis. The man walking towards her was the devil incarnate.

'Wow, he's coming over here,' Tracy announced over the pneumatic drill now shattering Louisa's eardrums. 'Oh-my-God! Isn't that Lord What's-his-name? You know—he was in your Britain's Most Eligible Bachelors list in the May issue. Maybe he's here to thank you.'

Hardly, Louisa thought bitterly. He'd already exacted his revenge for that list three months ago. Louisa's spine snapped straight and she folded her legs tightly under her chair. The tap of her high-heeled leather boot against the chair's stem sounded like the rat-a-tat-tat of a machine gun.

If he was here to take another cheap shot at her, he could forget it.

Louisa had seen him coming this time. He'd used her trusting nature, her innate flirtatiousness and her incendiary attraction to him against her three months ago. He would never catch her unawares again. This time she would fight back.

Luke Devereaux's long, purposeful strides ate up the acres of industrial blue carpeting as he zeroed in on his prey. He barely noticed the managing editor scuffling along at his heels, or the sea of female faces swivelling round to gawp at him. All his concentration, all his irritation, was focussed on one particular female. That she looked as stunningly beautiful as he remembered her—shiny gold-streaked hair framing an angelic face, killer cleavage accentuated by a figure-hugging dress covered in a bold Lichtenstein-like cartoon print, and mile-long legs encased in knee-high boots—only made him more determined to keep his cool.

Appearances were deceiving. This woman was no angel. What she was planning to do to him qualified as the worst thing a woman could do to a man.

Okay, things had got spectacularly out of hand three months ago. And he had to take a large part of the blame for that. The plan had been to teach her a little lesson about respecting people's privacy—not take advantage of her the way he had.

But she deserved a large part of the blame too. He'd never met anyone as reckless and impulsive before in his life. And he wasn't a saint. When a woman looked like her, smelt like her and felt like she did, what did she *think* he'd do? He couldn't imagine any bloke being able to think clearly under the same circumstances. How could he possibly have known she wasn't as experienced as she appeared?

Well, one thing was for sure: he was through feeling guilty about his part in it.

After his little chat with their mutual friend Jack

Devlin yesterday, all his guilt and all his regret over what had happened between them had given way to a slow-burning anger.

An innocent life was involved—and he'd do whatever he had to do to protect it.

Whatever hurts, whatever injustices he might have done her in the past, he had no qualms whatsoever about bending her to his will now. And the sooner she realised that, the better.

Louisa DiMarco was about to discover that Luke Devereaux never backed down from a fight.

What was it the late, unlamented Lord Berwick had said to him at their first and only meeting all those years ago? 'What doesn't kill you makes you stronger, boy.' He'd learnt that lesson the hard way when he was only seven years old. Frightened and alone, in a world he didn't know and didn't understand, he'd had to toughen up fast or go under. It was about time Miss DiMarco learnt the same lesson.

He reached Louisa's desk, saw the bright spark of fury in those stunning brown eyes, the smooth olive-toned skin mottled with temper and the elegant chin poked out in defiance. He imagined fisting his fingers in all those glorious blonde-brown curls and kissing her into submission.

To resist the urge he shoved his hands into his trouser pockets and kept his eyes flat and expressionless. It was a casual, predatory look that he knew terrorised his business opponents. Louisa, he noted, didn't even flinch.

The adrenalin rush he usually associated with a particularly tough new business challenge surged through his body. Teaching this woman how to face her responsibilities might actually be more of a pleasure than a pain. He was already anticipating the first lesson: getting Louisa to tell him what she should have told him weeks ago.

'Miss DiMarco, I want a word with you.'

CHAPTER TWO

I'LL just bet you do.

Louisa ignored Tracy's sharp intake of breath and looked her tormentor square in the eye.

'Excuse me, but who are you?' Louisa asked, as if she didn't know.

'This is Luke Devereaux, the new Lord Berwick,' Piers supplied, announcing the information as if he were introducing the king of the universe. 'Don't you remember? We featured him in May's Eligible Bachelors issue. He's the new owner of—'

Devereaux lifted a hand, halting Piers's sucking-up speech in mid-suck. 'Devereaux will do. I don't use the title,' he said, his eyes still boring into Louisa and his deep voice as annoyingly distinctive as she remembered it.

To think she'd once thought that accent—crisp British vowels underlaid with a lazy, measured cadence that sounded oddly American—and that steely, impenetrable gaze were sexy. Somebody must have spiked her drink with Viagra that night. His voice didn't sound compelling any more, just detached, while the icy blue-grey of his irises looked cold, not enigmatic.

All of which would explain why she was fighting the urge to shiver in the middle of August.

'I'm sure that's all very fascinating.' She flicked her hair back. 'But I'm afraid I'm terribly busy at the moment. And we only do one Eligible Bachelors issue a year. Maybe if you're still eligible next year you could come back, and I'll interview you then.'

Louisa congratulated herself on the deliberate insult. She knew how much he had despised being on her list. But she didn't get as much satisfaction as she'd hoped. Instead of looking annoyed, he simply stared at her. Not by a single flicker of his eyelashes did he acknowledge the hit. Then, to her silent irritation, his mouth curved at the edges. He put his hand flat on her desk and leaned over her. The familiar citrus scent of the soap he used had her boot-heel tapping harder against the chair.

'You want to have this discussion in public? That's fine by me,' he said, in a voice so low only she could hear it. 'But then I'm not the one who works here.'

She didn't have a clue what this was all about, but from his predatory smile she suspected the 'discussion' he intended to have would be personal. As much as she didn't want to give him any quarter, at the same time she didn't want to be humiliated in front of everyone she worked with.

'All right, then, Mr Devereaux,' she remarked loudly, swivelling to turn off her computer. 'As luck would have it, I might be able to squeeze in an interview now. I could talk to our features editor—maybe she'll consider putting it into next month's issue. You're obviously very keen to get your face out there, so the debutantes know what they're missing.'

He straightened away from her. One muscle in his cheek twitched. She'd got her hit that time.

'Which is not a lot,' she continued under her breath, going for the jackpot.

She didn't get it. The tension in his jaw disappeared and

he smiled. 'That's very accommodating of you, Miss DiMarco,' he said. 'Believe me, I'll make it worth your while.'

Ignoring the thinly veiled threat, Louisa turned to Tracy, who was doing a very good impression of a goldfish. 'I'll finish the article later, Trace. Tell Pam I should still make the five o'clock deadline.'

'You won't be back this afternoon,' Devereaux announced from behind her.

Louisa had swung round to correct him when Piers butted in. 'Mr Devereaux has asked that you take the rest of the day off. I've already approved it.'

'But I've got an article due today,' Louisa said, stunned. Piers was usually a total Nazi about copy deadlines.

He waved the remark away, looking harassed. 'Pam's going to stick in an extra page of ads. Your article can wait till next month. If Mr Devereaux needs you with him today we'll have to accommodate him.'

What? Since when did the managing editor of *Blush* magazine take orders from aristocratic bullies like Luke Devereaux?

Devereaux, who'd been listening to their conversation with apparent indifference, chose that moment to pick her bag up from the desk. 'Is this yours?' he asked impatiently.

'Yes,' Louisa replied, still disorientated. What was going on here?

He took her arm and tugged her out of her chair. 'Let's go,' he said, steering her out of the office with his hand clamped on her elbow.

She wanted to yank her arm out of his grip. She yearned to tell him where he could stick his Attila the Hun act. But everyone was staring at them. And Louisa would rather die than cause a scene in front of her colleagues. She was forced to submit to being marched out of the office and down the stairs like a disobedient schoolchild under the command of the headmaster.

It didn't stop her fuming every single step of the way.

By the time they'd walked out onto Camden High Street, Louisa's temper had reached boiling point. She wrestled her arm out of Devereaux's grasp. 'How dare you do that? Who do you think you are?'

He stopped by a flashy convertible sports car, parked in a no-parking zone at the front of the office. Opening the door, he flung Louisa's bag into the back seat. 'Get in the car.'

'I will not.' Of all the cheek! He was treating her as if she were one of his minions. Well, he could think again. Piers might obey his orders, but she most certainly did not. She crossed her arms over her chest, determined not to budge an inch.

His eyebrow lifted. 'Get in the car, Louisa,' he said, his voice deadly calm. 'Unless you want me to pick you up and put you in there.'

'You wouldn't dare.'

She had barely finished the sentence before she was hoisted off her feet. She had just enough time to gasp, and slap her fist against the solid wall of his chest, when she was dumped like a sack of potatoes into the passenger seat. The door slammed and the locks clicked shut. She shot up onto her knees, determined to climb right back out again. Unfortunately her movements were somewhat restricted by the skin-tight pencil skirt of her much-loved designer dress. She'd barely wriggled it up past her knees when the car peeled away from the kerb and she was thrown back against the seat.

'Put your belt on before you get hurt,' he shouted above the engine noise.

'Let me out. This is kidnapping!' The words came out on an outraged squeak, which would have been embarrassing if she hadn't been in a state of shock.

Handling the steering wheel with one hand, he reached across her with the other and pulled a pair of sunglasses out of the glove compartment. 'Stop being melodramatic,' he said, not even sparing her a glance as he put the glasses on.

'Me-lo-dra…!' She sputtered to a stop. No one but her father had ever treated her with such high-handedness. And she'd put a stop to that when she was a teenager. She certainly wasn't going to put up with it now. 'How dare you?'

He slowed the car to stop at a traffic light and turned to her, an annoyingly assured smile on his face. 'I think we've already established that I would dare. Now, if you want we can have another tussle—which you won't win,' he added with complete certainty. 'Or you can do what you're told and save a little of your precious dignity.'

Before she could think of a pithy enough reply, he'd shifted into First and accelerated across the intersection.

Drat, she'd missed her chance to leap out.

'Put your belt on.' He repeated the words as he shot up a side street, narrowly missing some ambling pedestrians.

Grudgingly she put the belt on—not quite angry enough yet to get killed for the sake of her pride. He'd have to stop eventually, and then she'd let him have it. Until then she'd give him the silent treatment.

That plan worked for about five minutes. But after they'd wound their way through the back streets of Camden, sped down the wide tree-lined outer circle of Regent's Park and crossed Euston Road into Bloomsbury, her curiosity had got the better of her.

'Where exactly are we going? If lowly little me is allowed to ask, that is.'

The quick smile he flashed suggested he found her sarcasm amusing. 'Lowly? You?'

She didn't dignify that with a reply. 'I have a right to know where you're taking me.' Forget sarcasm—he obviously didn't have the intelligence to process it.

He made one more turn, braked, and then backed into a parking space outside a six-storey Georgian terraced house. He switched off the engine and, slinging his arm over the steering wheel, angled his body towards her. His shoulders looked even broader than she remembered them in the expertly fitted linen jacket and white shirt. Intimidated despite herself, she had to force herself not to shrink back into the seat.

'We're here. The appointment's not for another—' he glanced at his watch '—ten minutes,' he announced, as if that explained everything.

She peered past him and read the street sign on the corner. 'What are we doing in Harley Street?'

The house he'd stopped in front of had an ornate brass plaque listing two doctors' names. That made sense. Harley Street was the domain of London's most exclusive private medical practitioners. But nothing else did. Why had he brought her here?

He took his sunglasses off, flung them into the back seat. 'Answer me one question,' he said, his voice tight with annoyance. 'Were you ever going to tell me about it?'

'Tell you about what?' Why was he looking at her as if she'd tried to steal the crown jewels and he'd caught her red-handed?

His gaze wandered down to her abdomen. She folded her arms, feeling oddly defensive.

Fierce grey eyes met hers. They looked colder than ever. 'About my child, of course. What else?'

CHAPTER THREE

'YOUR *what*? What child?' Had she just entered *The Twilight Zone*? 'Have you gone mad?'

Louisa turned to grab the door handle, determined to get out of the car before he started speaking in tongues or something.

His fingers clamped on her wrist. 'Don't act the innocent. I know about the pregnancy. I know about your mood swings, the supposed stomach bug you had a month ago, and the fact that you haven't had a period in months.' His eyes dipped to her breasts. 'And there's a few other giveaways I can see for myself.'

She wrestled her hand out of his grasp. 'What have you been doing? Staking out my toilet?'

'Jack told me.'

'Jack Devlin told you I was pregnant?' she shouted, past caring if the whole of Harley Street heard her.

The mention of her best friend Mel's husband was the last straw. She'd forgotten that Jack and Devereaux were friends. It was how she and Devereaux had met—at a dinner party at Mel's house. And now Jack had told Devereaux she was pregnant. Next time she saw Jack she would have to kill him.

'Not in so many words,' Devereaux said, impatience sharpening his voice. 'We were talking about Mel's pregnancy and he mentioned you. Seems Mel thinks you're pregnant but that you're keeping it a secret for some reason.'

Okay, now she would have to kill Mel too. 'Please tell me you didn't tell Jack about us.'

She'd been so humiliated she hadn't told anyone. Not even Mel, and she usually told Mel everything.

But how did you tell your best friend that you'd slept with a man on a first date, that you'd discovered how incredible, how amazing sex could really be, that for ten rosy minutes of afterglow you'd deluded yourself into thinking you'd found the love of your life—and then been brought crashing down to earth when you discovered the truth. That Mr Right was actually Mr Dead Wrong in disguise. That he wasn't the sexy, flirtatious, easy-going ordinary guy he'd pretended to be all evening, but rather a cold, manipulative, controlling member of the aristocracy, who'd seduced you for writing an article about him he didn't like.

Humiliation didn't even begin to cover it.

'I didn't talk to Jack about us,' he snarled. 'I was much more interested in hearing what he had to say about you.' He was looking at her as if he had a right to his anger.

Suddenly sick of him, and his attitude, and the whole stupid mess, Louisa knew she just wanted to get away from him. 'I'm not pregnant. Now, I've had enough of this idiotic conversation. I'm going back to work.' She tried to turn away from him, but he grasped her wrist again. 'Let go of me.'

'When did you have your last period?'

'I'm not answering that.'

She struggled. His fingers tightened on her wrist.

'You're not going anywhere until you do,' he said firmly.

She stopped struggling. This was ridiculous. What were they arguing about?

Dropping her head back on the seat, she let her hand go limp and closed her eyes against the bright cloudless August afternoon. She wasn't pregnant. All she had to do was convince him and he'd let her go. And then this whole horrible scene would be over. She'd never have to see him again.

Shielding her eyes, she rolled her head towards him. He looked as implacable and determined as ever. She tried to remember when her last period had been. A flush crept up her neck. Okay, maybe it had been a while ago. But she'd always had wildly irregular periods. It didn't mean a thing. And anyway, she had definitely had one since they'd made love. Plus she'd taken a home pregnancy test. She wasn't that stupid.

'I took a home pregnancy test. Just in case. And it was negative.' To her astonishment, instead of looking repentant, he narrowed his eyes.

'When did you take it?'

'I don't know. A few days afterwards.'

'And did you bother to read the instructions properly?'

'Enough to know it was negative,' she said firmly, the guilty blush spreading across her cheeks. Okay, she hadn't read all the small print—but did anyone?

'I thought not,' he said.

Indignation seared through her and she stiffened in her seat. 'Don't talk to me as if I'm an imbecile. I took the test. It was negative. Plus I've had a period since that night, so it's all academic anyway.' Even if her period had been a light one, it had been enough to put her mind at rest.

She tried to wrestle her wrist free again.

He held fast and his brows lowered ominously. 'That night was over three months ago, and you're telling me you've only had one period since?' Exasperation sharpened every word.

'So what? I have irregular periods.' The blush intensified. Why was she talking to this man about her menstrual cycle? And why was she going on the defensive? 'Read my lips,' she said. 'There is no child.' The possibility didn't even bear thinking about.

He looked at the silver Rolex on his wrist again. 'I've made you an appointment with the top obstetrician in the UK. She can start by doing a pregnancy test.'

'Who on earth do you think you are?'

'Quite possibly the father of your child,' he shot back without even blinking. 'The condom broke, Louisa,' he said. 'You know that.' He let go of her wrist at last and proceeded to count off his points on the fingers of one hand. 'You haven't had a period in months. You had what could easily have been a bout of morning sickness a few weeks back, and your breasts are definitely fuller. You're taking another pregnancy test. A proper one that you can't muck up.'

The comment about her breasts had the flush blazing across her chest like a brush fire. 'I'm not pregnant. And even if I were…' which she most definitely was not '…what makes you so sure you're the father? For all you know I could be a complete slapper. I could have slept with ten other guys since that night. I could have slept with twenty,' she finished on a note of bravado.

'Yeah, but you didn't,' he said, with such certainty she wanted to slap him.

'Oh, I see.' Did the man's ego know no bounds? 'You think you were so memorable you spoiled me for other guys.

Is that it?' She was prepared to lie through her teeth rather than let him know the truth. 'Believe me, you weren't.'

He huffed out a breath and stared out through the windshield. 'Stop pretending you're something you're not.' He turned back to her. Was that pity or regret she could see in his eyes? 'I knew the flirting was an act the minute I got inside you.'

The blood burned in her cheeks, but she forced herself to flick a contemptuous glance at his crotch. 'Right, so you've got radar down there, have you?'

He shook his head, gave a hollow laugh, but she was certain now the look in his eyes was pity. She hated him for it. 'I wish I did. I would never have made love to you that night if I'd known how innocent you were.'

'Well, isn't that noble of you?' she sneered back, only realising after the fact that she'd as good as agreed with him. 'There's no need to feel guilty on my account. I wasn't a virgin,' she said, trying to regain the ground.

'I know, but you were the next best thing.' He sighed again. 'I'm sorry for what happened that night. I figured you knew the score. I didn't mean to hurt you.'

Yes, you did, she thought bitterly, but didn't say it. This was all too personal. If he saw how vulnerable she was, it would only humiliate her more.

'I'm sure this heart-to-heart is all very touching. But it doesn't change the fact that we've got nothing left to discuss.'

'We'll decide that once you've had the pregnancy test.'

The he-who-shall-be-obeyed tone was back.

She could have argued with him. She probably should have. But she felt unbearably weary all of a sudden, and over-emotional. She just wanted to get this over with now. So she never, ever had to see this man again.

Submitting to a quick pregnancy test seemed like a rela-

tively small price to pay. And she was already relishing
exactly what she was going to say to him when it turned
up negative.

CHAPTER FOUR

'CONGRATULATIONS, Miss DiMarco, you're pregnant.'

Louisa's heartbeat kicked so hard in her chest she thought she might be having a heart attack. She gaped at Dr Lester's encouraging smile, her hands fisting on the arms of her chair.

Forget *The Twilight Zone*—she'd just entered an alternative reality. She couldn't possibly have heard that right. 'Excuse me, what did you say?' Her voice sounded small and far away. Appropriate, really, seeing as it was coming from another dimension.

'You're expecting a baby, my dear.' The doctor glanced down at the test results, which had taken about ten minutes to come through from the on-site lab. 'In fact it's a very strong positive. From the hormone levels I'd say you're at least three months pregnant. Either that, or you're expecting twins.'

Louisa's hands started to shake. She gripped the chair even harder, worried she might collapse in a heap on the floor.

'Can you tell us the due date?' Devereaux asked from beside her.

Louisa looked at him in a daze. She'd forgotten he was even there.

She hadn't objected to him coming in with her to get the results. This was supposed to be her big I-told-you-so moment. She would have put up much more of a fight if she'd known what he would actually be witnessing was her life going in to freefall. He didn't look smug, though, or particularly overjoyed with his victory. He looked calm and in complete control. His reaction, if he'd even had one, had been carefully masked. It almost made her wish for smug.

'How about we do a quick ultrasound scan?' the doctor replied. 'We've got the equipment in the next room. We can check how the baby's doing and give you a more exact date.'

'Don't be silly—there is no baby.' Louisa cleared her throat, tried to halt the panic making her tongue go numb. 'You must have made a mistake. I'm not pregnant. I took a pregnancy test myself. And I had a period…' She paused. He would know how inexperienced she really was if she continued. Looking at the doctor's encouraging smile, it occurred to her that what he did or didn't know about her lack of a sex life since that night was probably academic now. And why should she care anyway? She forced herself to continue. 'I haven't been with anyone else since.'

The doctor sat down at her desk and steepled her fingers. 'What brand of home pregnancy test did you use and when did you take it?'

'I don't…' She hesitated, tried to remember, but all she could think about was how relieved she'd been when the stick had stayed clear. 'I'm not sure about the brand. But I took the test about a week, or maybe a bit less, after we…' She swallowed. This was hideous. 'After our night together.' She'd been frantic, after all.

'Okay,' Dr Lester said gently. 'Some home test kits are very sensitive. Others aren't. And they can give you what's called a false negative if you take them too soon. Now.' She propped her elbows on her desk, gave Louisa an enquiring look. 'How heavy was the period you had, and when did it occur after intercourse?'

Louisa realised her face was probably vermilion by now. 'Maybe a week or two afterwards, and it was fairly light.'

'What you had was spotting. Not uncommon around the time of implantation.'

'I thought you could only get pregnant in the middle, during ovulation.' It was another of the reasons she had been sure she wasn't pregnant.

The doctor simply smiled. 'Fertilisation can occur at any time, my dear. Especially if the couple are young or exceptionally fertile.'

The blood pumped into her cheeks and spread out across her neck.

'Does the spotting mean there could be harm to the baby?' Devereaux said.

Louisa kept her eyes on the doctor, determined not to even look at him. The whole situation suddenly felt surreal. As if she were having an out-of-body experience. How could she be pregnant by this man? She who hadn't intended to even *think* about the possibility of having children for at least another ten years. She was only twenty-six. She'd worked so hard to get where she was. Killed herself at school to take her A-levels a year early. Had slaved in odd jobs to pay her way through university, done night shifts and overtime at *London Nights* to establish herself in the mostly male world of local reporting, and then finally fled from the 'anything for a story' ethos to establish herself as a features writer on *Blush*. She was proud of what she'd achieved. *Blush* was a brilliantly written magazine that didn't just concern itself with the things that made women look and feel good, but also with the whole realm of the female experience. Now all that was in jeopardy because she'd made a foolish, reckless mistake. She'd fallen for a man who not only didn't care a hoot about her, but had the sperm of a prize-winning bull.

Fantastic, Louisa, you've really topped yourself this time.

'Don't worry about the spotting, Lord Berwick,' the doctor said indulgently. 'I'm sure your baby is fine. As I said, the test results show the pregnancy is firmly established. But I think an ultrasound scan will put everyone's mind at rest.' She smiled at Louisa, who was still processing the 'your baby' comment. 'Why don't you go through to the ultrasound suite, Miss DiMarco? It's right next door.'

After that little speech Louisa was surprised the woman had even put a question mark at the end of her sentence. It was clear the good doctor knew who was paying the bill. Louisa debated refusing to submit to the procedure. She slanted a look at Devereaux, who was watching her, his mouth set in a thin line of determination.

Not just the sperm of a bull, but the stubbornness to match.

She gave a heavy sigh. 'All right,' she said, standing up.

She walked to the door the doctor had indicated on watery legs.

Maybe there was still a small chance that this was all a hideous mistake, and when the doctor got her ultrasound equipment out she wouldn't find a baby after all.

'There's the head and the spine,' the doctor said enthusiastically, pointing at the sepia-toned three-dimensional image.

'That's incredible,' Devereaux said in hushed tones. 'It's so clear.'

'We have the newest, most state-of-the-art equipment here. We're very proud of...'

Louisa tuned out their conversation, transfixed by the bright, incandescent image.

The coolness of the gel on her skin, the press of the ultrasound wand, even the rapid ticks of the baby's heartbeat being monitored by the machinery faded into oblivion as Louisa stared at the tiny arms and legs, the large head, the perfectly formed little body.

I'm looking at my baby.

The words flickered in her consciousness, and then a dizzying sense of awe surged through the dense fog of self-pity.

The doctor adjusted the wand and then tapped a few buttons. A close-up of the baby's face appeared as if by magic. Its eyes were closed, one tiny little fist covering its nose and mouth.

'What's it doing?' Louisa heard her voice coming from miles away.

The doctor laughed. 'Why, I think it's trying to suck its thumb.'

Oh, God, oh, God, oh, God.

Tears stung Louisa's eyes and she tried to blink them back. All this time she'd been thinking about herself, about how this whole situation was going to affect her, when there was a much more important life at stake—that of her child.

The baby hadn't seemed real until this moment, but now guilt engulfed her. Whatever her problems with Devereaux—however much this pregnancy would change her life, her dreams—she would never regret the miracle growing inside her. But she'd be bringing this perfect little person into the world without any of the things she herself had taken for granted—a loving two-parent home, a stable family life.

As it always did, thoughts of her childhood brought back memories of her mother. Louisa let out a shaky sigh. If only she could talk to her mother now, just one more time. She trembled, the echo of long-remembered grief making the tears spill over her lids and run down her face. She reached up to wipe her cheeks, but strong fingers took hold of her wrist.

She looked up to see Devereaux staring down at her from his seat beside the couch, his expression unreadable in the darkened room. He pulled a handkerchief out of his back pocket and dabbed at her hairline, then skimmed the clean-smelling linen across her temples. When he'd finished, he put the handkerchief in her hand and closed his fist around her shaking fingers.

He squeezed and let go. 'You okay?' he asked quietly.

Hardly, she thought, but sniffed, burying her nose in his handkerchief to buy time. All she needed now was for him to be nice to her and she'd turn into a gibbering wreck.

'Yes, of course,' she said, as soon as she could speak, struggling to sound as matter-of-fact as possible while her insides were turning to mush.

He watched her a moment longer, those steely eyes giving absolutely nothing away, then turned back to the doctor, who was busy fiddling with her state-of-the-art equipment.

'Right, I've checked all the vital organs and everything seems to be developing well,' the doctor said at last, swinging round to address them both. 'I must say the foetus is a little long for dates.' She smiled benignly at Louisa, then spoke to Devereaux. 'Can I ask how tall you are, Lord Berwick?'

'Call me Luke,' he said absently. 'I'm six-three.'

'That explains it, then,' the doctor said, putting the ultrasound wand back in its holder. She wiped the remaining gel off Louisa's belly and then gave her an indulgent smile.

'As long as Miss DiMarco's sure she couldn't have conceived a week or so earlier?'

Try three years, Louisa thought grimly.

'The baby's mine,' Devereaux said with absolute certainty, before Louisa had a chance to answer. 'It was conceived on the twenty-fifth of May.'

Louisa's fingers clutched the robe as she wrapped it around her abdomen, all her soft feelings towards him squashed flat. He really was the most arrogant man on the planet. She wanted to tell him where he could shove his assumptions, but she couldn't. Unfortunately he was right. The beautiful little human being on the screen in front of her was his child.

Louisa sucked in a deep breath, let it out slowly.

As the doctor began to waffle on about due dates, percentile growth scales and antenatal vitamins, Louisa watched Devereaux listening to the doctor's instructions, his harshly handsome face illuminated by the frozen image of their baby.

Their baby.

She sighed and stared at the screen again. The child growing in her womb meant that no matter what she did, no matter where she went, she would always have a connection to this man. This demanding, domineering, ruthless man who had hurt her so terribly once. A man who had tricked her into thinking he was the man of her dreams and then made her feel like a fool.

Exactly what kind of father had she given her unborn child?

Tears clogged her throat again. She couldn't think about that now; it was too big a question to contemplate and far too soon to worry about it. She gulped the tears down hastily.

How ironic, though, that the most incredible, the most amazing moment of her life had also turned out to be the most devastating. Now she knew how David must have felt when he was aiming his pea-shooter at Goliath.

CHAPTER FIVE

LUKE shifted into second gear to take the turn into Regent's Park and glanced at the woman sitting silently in the passenger seat. Only the high curve of her cheekbone was visible behind the glossy curtain of hair. The burnished blonde highlights haloed round her head in the sunshine. She'd been staring out the window for the last ten minutes. Not only that, but she'd said barely three words since they'd left the ultrasound suite.

It was starting to worry him.

From his short association with Louisa DiMarco he knew she wasn't the quiet type. On their one and only date he'd been captivated by her bright, sharply witty and pretty much non-stop chatter despite himself. Of course he'd witnessed a much sharper side to her tongue once he'd told her who he was. But he'd still prefer those rapier-sharp barbs to this oppressive silence.

He pressed his foot on the accelerator. The park had a twenty-mile-per-hour speed limit, but at three o'clock on a Friday afternoon, and with the weathermen forecasting glorious sunshine across the country for the whole weekend, the sweltering city was already deserted.

As the majestic avenue of oak and maple trees whisked

past, the dappled shade bringing some respite from the after-noon heat, Luke contemplated Louisa's reaction. Maybe her silence was a blessing in disguise. He needed a chance to regroup, reanalyse the situation, rethink his position as well.

In all the time he'd spent brooding since yesterday—his resentment building at her irresponsible behaviour—it had never even occurred to him that she might not know she was expecting a child. Weren't women supposed to have a sixth sense about this sort of thing?

But she'd had absolutely no clue—no inkling. As she'd lain on the doctor's couch, looking fragile in the oversized robe, the naked shock on her face had been genuine.

'Where are we going?' she asked from beside him, inter-rupting his train of thought. She still wasn't looking at him.

'To your place,' he said.

She turned, then, looking mildly surprised. 'Do you remember where it is?'

He nodded, not quite able to speak as he took in the stunning face that he could now admit had been lodged in his brain for twelve agonising weeks—the rich chocolate-brown eyes, the full lips, the high cheekbones and the honey-toned skin that he knew tasted as sweet as it looked.

He remembered every detail from that night—not just her address. The chilly spring air as they had strolled through Regent's Park after leaving Mel and Jack's. The feel of her warm, lush young body pressed against his side. The fresh scent of the petal blossom that had blown over them in the breeze. Her captivating laughter when she'd tried to catch it as she danced down the path in front of him, her arms outstretched. The rich taste of the late-night cap-puccino they'd shared on Camden High Street, and the flir-tatious way she'd licked the milky foam off her lips.

And even more devastating than those memories were the ones that had come after.

Her arms clinging around his neck as he carried her into her tiny flat. The taste of her mouth on his—strong coffee and sultry innocence—as he bared her breasts in the cramped hallway. Those shocked sobs she'd given as he'd stroked her to her first climax, and then the feel of her, tight as a velvet fist around him, as he rocked them both to a brutal, devastating finish.

Yes, he remembered a lot more than just her address.

She stared out the window again. 'I need to go back to the office, actually. I'd appreciate it if you'd drop me there.'

'I'm taking you to Havensmere.' He might have to rethink a few things, but his main plan was still solid. 'We're only stopping at your place to pick up your stuff.'

Her head whipped round, her eyes darkening to a vivid black. He braced himself, more than ready for the on-slaught.

Louisa's insides were still pretty much mush, but the indignation sprinting up her backbone gave her energy levels a considerable boost. 'You know what, Devereaux? I don't have to do what you tell me. So you'd better get over that little delusion right now.'

She watched him brake at the lights. His eyes flicked to her waist. 'Under the circumstances, you should call me Luke,' he said calmly.

'I'll call you what I like, Devereaux.' It was petty and rude, and she knew it, but she didn't want to call him Luke. She'd called him Luke that night.

He didn't rise to the challenge, didn't even bother to reply, but left her fuming until he whipped the car onto her street and parked a few doors down from her flat.

'You're tired and you're over-emotional,' he said, in the same measured tone that so infuriated her. 'You've had a shock. I understand that.'

He certainly had a lot to learn about her, she thought, if he figured accusing her of being virtually hysterical was going to calm her down. She crossed her arms and fumed in stony silence.

'I don't want to fight with you about this,' he continued. 'But we've got a lot to discuss, and Havensmere is where we're going to do it.'

She straightened, uncrossing her arms and bracing them on the seat, ready for battle. 'Don't you get it? I don't want to go anywhere with you.'

He pushed the thick hair off his brow, pulled the key out of the ignition and gave a heavy sigh. 'I know.'

For the first time she noticed the lines of fatigue around his eyes. When he looked at her she noticed something else—something that surprised her. Was that concern? Had he been as deeply affected by today's events as she had? she wondered.

'Whether we like it or not,' he continued, his tone rigid, 'we've made a child together, and we're going to have to deal with the consequences. You need to lose the hostility. It's counterproductive.'

Good grief, he'd done it again. Just when she was starting to feel ever so slightly sympathetic towards him, he'd made her mad. It was as if he had an innate skill for winding her up. But she held on to the caustic retort that wanted to spit out.

Something he'd said had sent a tremor of fear skidding down her spine. What did he mean by 'dealing with the consequences'? He was rich, influential, and he'd already taken the initiative with her medical treatment. She'd been in a trance back at the doctor's office, but she had heard him setting up another appointment with the receptionist.

Was he even now planning to pressure her into an abortion?

The thought that he might not want this baby should have made her angry, but instead it made her feel unbearably sad—and bone-sappingly weary. The brief spurt of temper that had sustained her fizzled out.

As much as she hated to admit it, he was right about a few things. She *was* tired and over-emotional—and frankly in shock. All of which meant she was in no fit state to argue with him now—a man who was obviously an expert at getting his own way. She needed to get a decent night's sleep first—marshal her forces. Going to his stately home in Wiltshire would buy her some time in that regard.

But there was one thing she wanted to get clear before she gave in to any more of his demands.

'Frankly, I find your patronising, pushy behaviour "counterproductive". Maybe if you stopped treating me as if you owned me, I'd "lose the hostility".' Well, a bit of it, at any rate.

His eyebrow shot up, and she could see he wasn't pleased with her assessment of his character. His jaw hardened as he controlled his response.

The muscle twitching in his cheek brought on a brutal flash of memory from that night. He'd looked exactly the same when he'd been buried inside her, filling her unbearably, desperately holding back his orgasm while her body burst into flames. The physical reaction that followed the blast of memory shocked Louisa into silence. Her thigh muscles loosened, her nipples hardened and she felt a long liquid pull low in her belly that could only mean one thing.

Arousal.

She clenched her thigh muscles, wrapped her arms round her waist. What was wrong with her? He'd used her, hurt her, and now he was about to try and force her to abort her baby and still her body yearned for him.

Ignore it.

'What's wrong?' His deep, urgent voice reached her through the turmoil. 'Are you sick?'

Louisa forced the panic down. 'I'm fine,' she murmured.

He brushed his fingertip down her cheek. 'You look pale. Are you still suffering from morning sickness ?'

She pulled away from the electric touch. 'No.' She certainly wasn't feeling sick at the moment. Far from it.

She took in the frown on his face and noticed the clean, lemony scent of his soap. Of course. That was it. The sudden jolt of desire had to be the pregnancy hormones mucking about with her libido. Hadn't she read somewhere that pregnant women responded instinctively to the scent of their child's father? Something to do with pheromones? The panic edged back and she eased the death grip of her arms around her midriff. She wasn't attracted to him. It was just some weird chemical reaction. But as she tried to relax in her seat her erogenous zones continued to rebel.

'I have staff at the house,' he said, watching her intently. 'The place has close to sixty rooms and over a hundred acres of grounds. We'll have the time, space and privacy we need to discuss this properly and make the necessary arrangements.'

'I'm not in the mood to talk tonight,' she blurted out, panic seizing her at the thought of what he might mean by 'necessary arrangements'.

His lips lifted in a wry grin and she realised she'd just agreed to go. 'That's okay,' he said. 'Neither am I. But I want to drive down tonight, and I'd like you to come with me.' He hesitated. 'Please.'

After her ridiculous reaction to him Louisa wasn't so sure agreeing to spend the weekend with him was the smart choice, but the look in his eyes when he said please tipped the balance. She had the distinct impression it wasn't a word he was all that familiar with. That he'd said it to her made her feel as if she'd won some monumental victory. Added to that, exhaustion was beginning to settle over her like a heavy blanket. She didn't have the strength to argue with him. 'Okay, I'll come. But only for one night.'

He nodded, got out of the car. She bent to gather her bag. He'd walked around the car and whisked the passenger door open before she had a chance to do it herself. He took her elbow as she stepped out. She dismissed the flutter in her stomach at his gallantry. She'd been fooled into thinking his good manners meant something once before.

He fell into step beside her as she walked to the Georgian terraced house where she rented the top-floor flat.

'You should wait by the car,' she said. The last thing she wanted was for him to come into her flat. The memories of that night were far too fresh already. 'You'll get a parking ticket if you don't have a permit.'

He didn't even break stride. 'I'll risk it.'

She stopped at the door, fiddled with the strap of her bag. He was going to make her say it. 'I'd like to get my stuff alone, if you don't mind. I'd prefer you didn't come up to the flat.'

He studied her for several agonising seconds. 'All right, I'll wait here,' he said, then tucked his forefinger under her chin. He stroked his thumb along her jaw. 'But don't be too long.'

She twisted her head away, disturbed by the sizzle of sensation the slight touch had caused. 'I'll take as long as I like, Devereaux.'

As a parting shot it wasn't great, but it would have to do.

She stomped into the house and tried to concentrate on her irritation as she tramped wearily up the two flights of stairs to her flat. But as she threw some clothes and toiletries into an overnight bag she found she couldn't block out the residual hum of arousal making her ache.

Louisa locked the front door to the house and picked up her overnight bag with a tired sigh. She spied Devereaux leaning on his flashy car, his butt perched on the glossy black paintwork and his face in profile as he spoke quietly into his mobile phone. From this distance she couldn't hear what he was saying, but with his legs crossed at the ankles, his shirtsleeves rolled up and his sunglasses on he looked relaxed and confident. The thought made Louisa's temper kick in at last. Here she was, facing the biggest, scariest, most awe-inspiring challenge of her life, and the man responsible was conducting business as usual. Her world had changed beyond all recognition in the space of an afternoon and he looked as if he didn't have a care in the world. The fact that he looked so dashing, the insouciant pose accentuating his tall, lean build and the August sunshine highlighting that dramatic face and the perfectly cut waves of dark hair, only pushed Louisa's temper further over the edge. How could he look so composed when she felt as if she'd been through an emotional wringer in the last hour?

Bolstering her exhaustion with resentment, Louisa

marched to the car, her boot heels clacking on the pavement like a warning volley.

'We'll probably get there around eight,' Luke said to his housekeeper. 'Prepare the adjoining suite. I'll see you in a couple of hours, Mrs Roberts.' He ended the call and turned to watch Louisa's approach, alerted by the harsh click of her heels in the summer stillness. With her head held high, her eyes boring holes into him and her hips swaying enticingly in the skimpy dress, she looked like an enraged Amazon.

He considered it a big improvement on fragile and exhausted.

He pushed away from the car, ready and willing to handle whatever she might want to throw at him.

'All set?' he said, in a deliberately neutral voice.

Her eyes flashed hot. 'Here.' She thrust a small leather holdall at him, then marched round to the passenger side. 'Let's get this over with, then,' she said, jerking open the door and getting in.

He dumped her bag in the back and got in too. 'I thought we agreed to ditch the hostility?' he said mildly, turning on the ignition and pulling the car out onto the street.

'Oh, did we? I must have missed that command. Sorry.'

Temper suited her, he thought. It gave her cheeks a becoming glow, made the caramel colour of her eyes even more striking, and had her glorious bosom heaving in a way that was—well, distracting.

He couldn't help it. He chuckled.

'Do you think this is funny?' she demanded, as outraged as she was incredulous.

Luke stifled a laugh. She was right, it was hardly appropriate in the circumstances, but still he couldn't resist saying, 'You look great when you're angry. I thought so that first night and I think so now.'

'If that's your cock-eyed idea of a compliment, I pity any woman unfortunate enough to get involved with you.'

'Like you, you mean?' he asked lightly, letting the insult pass.

'One quickie does not an involvement make,' she snapped.

'As I recall it wasn't quick.'

She didn't say a word as he stopped at the set of traffic lights leading onto the Westway. He pressed the button on the dash to raise the convertible's roof.

'I don't want to talk about that night,' she said at last. The temper seemed to have drained out of her. Luke had to strain to hear her over the hydraulic hum. 'I've been trying to forget it for the last three months,' she finished.

'Sounds like you've had about as much luck with that as I have,' he said gently. He could see confusion and panic in her gaze when she turned to look at him. It gave him the leverage he needed. 'I guess there'll be no forgetting it now. For either of us.'

She sighed. 'I suppose not. But that doesn't mean we have to repeat the same mistake twice.'

Until she'd said the words, issued the challenge, it hadn't even occurred to Luke how much he *wanted* to repeat their so-called mistake.

Yes, he found her incredibly attractive. Yes, she tantalised him as much as she infuriated him. And, yes, he hadn't been able to forget her. But after the way their night together had ended he'd decided not to pursue her. He wasn't a masochist.

But as she sat in his car, watching him—her chin stuck out, her eyes wary, her bottom lip trembling just enough to give her away—he knew he'd been fooling himself. It wasn't just Jack's offhand comments during their weekly game of squash that had got him clearing his calendar for the week, calling Harley Street and then storming into her office this afternoon. And it wasn't the flickering image of their baby in the doctor's surgery either.

He still wanted her. In fact he'd never stopped wanting her, and it was about time he admitted it.

When he'd seen the baby on the ultrasound screen there had been shock, sure, but right along with it had been a wave of masculine satisfaction that he couldn't explain.

This baby was going to complicate his life. No question about it. He was no romantic fool, and he wasn't a family man either. He didn't even know what family meant. So why, on some elemental level, was he pleased about this pregnancy?

The answer was painfully obvious. His reaction to the baby—to his baby, he now realised—had been instinctive and purely male. With her carrying his child she was bound to him in a way she hadn't been before. He'd stamped his claim on her in the most basic, primitive way possible.

From her combative behaviour this afternoon, though, he could see persuading her of this simple fact was going to take patience, single-mindedness and a degree of ruthlessness.

It was a good thing he had plenty of all three.

'What happened that night wasn't a mistake,' he said, punching the accelerator as they drove up the ramp onto the elevated motorway out of town. 'Not for me and certainly not for you. Or did you want to spend the rest of your life faking your orgasms?'

Louisa sucked in a shocked breath as his terse comment sliced right through her defences.

She'd told him that in confidence. How could he bring it up now?

The urge to punch him was so strong she began to shake.

She wanted to ignore his asinine remark and the memories it triggered. But as she swallowed down the hot ball of humiliation that surged up her throat the memories came flooding back anyway.

CHAPTER SIX

Three months earlier

'How much further is it to your flat? It's getting chilly,' Luke declared, squeezing Louisa's shoulders.

She snuggled into the embrace. He felt so solid, so good, so right beside her.

'Stop moaning,' she teased. 'It's a beautiful night.' But then the fresh spring breeze ruffled her hair and made her shiver.

'You're cold,' he said. 'Here.'

He pulled off his jacket and draped it over her, then gave her arms a vigorous rub. Well, that had certainly warmed her right up.

'Come on,' he said, slinging his arm back over her shoulders. 'Let's grab a cab and I'll take you home.'

She could smell the hint of his soap, feel the warmth of his skin on the well-worn leather jacket. She stared at his profile as he scanned Camden High Street, looking for a cab, and knew that she didn't want this evening to end. Not ever.

They climbed into the cab. She bent forward to give the driver directions. As she finished talking, warm hands clamped around her waist. 'Come here.'

'Oh!' She gasped as she landed on his lap.

He wrapped his arms around her, anchoring her in place. 'How do you feel about necking in the back seat of a cab?' he whispered, nuzzling her ear.

Her bangles jingled as she threaded her fingers through the hair at his nape. 'I'm all for it.' His thigh muscles tensed beneath her bottom. 'But unfortunately it'll only take about two minutes to get there.'

'That's a shame,' he whispered, but she could sense the smile on his lips as they touched hers.

Her mouth opened instinctively. He tasted of coffee and barely leashed passion as his tongue probed. Delicious little shock waves pulsed through her body, and her fingers trembled on his neck as the kiss deepened.

Framing her face, he broke away first. 'We'd better stop,' he murmured, his voice strained. 'Two minutes isn't going to be nearly long enough.'

Even in the dim light of the cab she could see his eyes had gone dark with arousal, the pupils so dilated the silvery-grey of his irises had all but disappeared.

A reckless thrill shimmered through her body, the solid ridge pressing against her bottom making her insides go all tingly. 'Why don't you come in for a coffee?' she said.

The bold offer shocked her a little. She adored flirting—the long looks and secret touches, the sensual hum of anticipation—but over the years she'd become very discerning about taking it any further. For the simple reason that sex had always been such a huge disappointment.

At twenty-six she'd never had anything even approaching an orgasm. She'd stopped kissing frogs a few years back, because, frankly, faking her enjoyment had got old really fast. But despite that, in some small corner of her heart, she'd always known that she'd get her bells and whistles when she found her Mr Right.

Tonight, when she'd been introduced to Luke in Mel's living room, his thick wavy hair falling over dark brows and the penetrating look in his smoky eyes making her pulse skitter, her heart had whispered, *Could this be him?*

They'd hit it off instantly, and become so absorbed in each other they'd virtually ignored the other dinner guests. Then he'd offered to walk her home. As they'd strolled through Regent's Park together—the sky dusky with twilight, pink blossoms scenting the air and the comforting weight of his arm around her keeping her warm—everything had been so perfectly romantic, the connection between them so clear, she'd had no trouble at all convincing herself Prince Charming had finally put in an appearance. This potent zing of arousal was just the icing on the cake.

He frowned in the shadows, his hands slipping down to her shoulders. 'Are you sure you want to ask me in?'

'You don't want to?' Her heart stuttered. Wasn't this where they had been headed all evening?

He gave a half-laugh, the sound pained. 'Of course I do. But I should tell you…' He paused. His thumb drew a lazy circle on her bare collarbone under the lapel of his jacket, making her skin burn. 'Once we're in your flat I won't be all that interested in coffee.'

'Phew, that's a relief,' she said, her heart pummelling. 'Because I'm not even sure I've got any.'

He laughed softly. 'I'm glad we got that settled,' he said, nipping her earlobe as the taxi shuddered to a halt outside her house. Any reservations she had left dissolved in a liquid pool of lust.

He paid the driver as she stepped out of the cab, then

led her up the front steps of the Georgian terraced house she indicated, his hand swinging in hers.

She had to scrabble around in her bag to find her keys, the ripples of excitement making her fumble.

'Let me,' he said calmly, and took the keys to unlock the heavy oak door.

He pushed the door open and stepped back so she could precede him. Her heart melted at the instinctive courtesy. All evening he'd been opening doors for her, holding out her chair, paying the tab without asking. On their next date she would offer to pay her share. After all, she was a modern and liberated woman. But she had to admit his macho, take-charge chivalry tonight had made her feel special—precious, even—and even more aroused.

He grasped her hand as soon as they were through the front door and took charge again, striding towards the stairwell. 'Which floor?' he asked.

'The top one.' The words came out on a sigh of regret. 'Let's hurry,' she said, pulling her hand out of his to run up the stairs ahead of him.

'Hey, wait for me.' He chuckled, catching up with her easily as his long legs took the stairs two at a time.

Despite taking two step classes a week at the local gym, Louisa couldn't catch her breath by the time they reached her flat—which probably had more to do with the weight of his hand on the small of her back than with physical exertion.

She found her keys again, but couldn't find the lock in the darkness, as his fingers trailed over her nape. He pushed the heavy weight of her hair to one side and his lips nibbled across the back of her neck. The keys clattered onto the floor.

He laughed and bent to pick them up. 'We better get this open,' he said softly, 'before we get carried away.'

The front door duly opened, she gasped as he swept her into his arms to carry her over the threshold. His handsome face looked determined in the dim light, his harsh breathing matching her own. She clung on to his neck and tried to stop shivering. If she got much more excited she'd pass out and ruin everything.

He let her down slowly. The wide flowing skirt of her dress rode up, the bare skin of her legs brushing the stiff new denim of his jeans. Her back bumped against the wall as his hand stroked up her thigh.

'You've been driving me wild all evening,' he mumbled as his lips skimmed the sensitive skin under her ear. 'I want you so much.' His voice shook with an urgency that both shocked and thrilled her. 'Tell me you feel the same,' he demanded.

'Yes.' She choked out the word, dragging him closer as his hands explored her inner thigh. His thumb traced the edge of her panties and then his fingers pulled the lace aside and plunged into the wet heat. She sobbed, quivering, unable to believe the sensations as he circled and rubbed at the heart of her. The licks of flame flared into a raw, molten heat.

She tensed, grasped his arm, bucking under his stroking fingers as the flames burned hotter, shocked by the intensity. 'Please—don't. It's too much,' she cried, sure she was about to leap over some unknown precipice and shatter into a million jagged pieces.

'Shh…' His fingers slowed, retreating slightly. 'Let go, Louisa,' he said, his voice coaxing. 'It'll be good, I promise.'

He flicked over the nub again, and she jerked as the consuming heat seared through her.

'I can't,' she said, embarrassment warring with need. He must think she was mad, but she couldn't do it. She couldn't let go and risk plummeting into the unknown. Her thigh muscles tensed even more. She sucked in a breath, humiliation tightening her throat.

What a great time to find out she was frigid—when her own personal Prince Charming had his hand down her knickers.

'Just relax a minute,' he said, his fingers still circling lazily, but mercifully not touching The Spot. She could see the small lines round his eyes in the half-light. Was he smiling at her? Did he think she was funny? Or, worse, inadequate?

She shrank back. Oh, this was hideous. She'd never felt more exposed in her life. 'Maybe we should take a rain-check on the coffee?' she whispered, her chest imploding as she tried to wriggle out of his embrace.

He drew his hand up and placed it on her hip, trapping her. 'What's the matter?' he asked.

'I'm not in the mood any more,' she said, staring at his chest.

He tucked his forefinger under her chin, lifted her gaze to his. 'You were so close, and then you tensed up. What happened?'

She shook her head, chewed her bottom lip to stop it trembling. 'Does it matter?' she murmured, utterly devastated.

He cupped her face in his palm, ran his thumb across her cheekbone. Her heart clutched tight. The tenderness, the understanding she saw in his face, made her want to weep.

'Of course it matters,' he said. 'Look, all you need to do is relax.' His hands settled on her shoulders, massaged the rigid muscles. 'You're all knotted up,' he said, firm fingers digging into the knots. 'No wonder you couldn't come.'

Slowly, very slowly, as his fingers worked their magic,

kneading her shoulders, skimming up and down her neck, the tight balls of muscle began to release. He kissed her jaw, found her mouth, and on a long breathless sigh she let him in. Warmth flowed between her thighs.

His thumbs brushed over her breasts. Her nipples tightened at the slight touch.

'You see—you can do it,' he said, satisfaction deepening his voice.

He kissed her again, his tongue delving deep now, possessing her as he pushed his jacket off her shoulders.

'I want to see you, Louisa,' he murmured as he stepped back.

She let him tug the bodice of her dress down and undo her bra, glad of the comforting shadows. Her chest heaved as he pulled the pink lace away, baring her to his gaze. His fingers stroked the top of her breasts as he stared at them, and she shivered.

She should feel exposed, embarrassed. She was practically naked, after all, and he was still fully dressed. But as his eyes met hers the stormy grey glittered with appreciation and she felt need twist and clutch in her belly.

He bent his head and lifted the peak to his lips. He licked, and then teased the hard bud with his teeth until it went rigid with desire. At last he took the nipple in his mouth and gave it the strong suction she craved. She swayed as pleasure battered her in slow, slumberous waves. Then he turned his attention to her other breast, subjecting it to the same delicious torture. Small sobs clogged her throat as she slid into the hoped-for oblivion.

'Okay, let's get to the heart of the matter,' he whispered. His breath feathered the wet flesh of her breasts as he dipped to hook his fingers in the waistband of her panties and drag them down. She stepped out of them, her legs shaking.

He lifted the hem of her dress and cupped her sex, pressing the heel of his palm against her.

She fisted her hands in his hair, dragged him to her for a fervent, thankful kiss. He kept her suspended for ever, it seemed. The desire grew, the anticipation mounting to impossible proportions as his hand rubbed and the soft cotton of his T-shirt brushed against her swollen nipples. She moved her hips, trying to push herself into his palm. At long last his fingers sank into the slick folds, seeking, tempting. She jerked as he touched The Spot, the sensation electric.

'Don't panic,' he murmured. 'We're going to take it slowly this time.'

He began an inspired rhythm, stroking and then retreating, until she was hyperventilating for real. But this time she was drawn to the brutal precipice, happy to race towards it and fling herself over. She soared free, sobbing out her release as her whole body splintered apart in a glorious, pyrotechnic explosion.

'You see? That wasn't so hard, was it?' he said, his voice teasing as she buried her head in his neck, her body shaking with the final throes of orgasm.

He smelt delicious, she thought, as a great big silly grin spread across her face. So that was how it was done! She felt as if she'd just conquered the universe.

He framed her face in his hands, looked into her eyes. 'How about we do that again? Together this time?'

'Sounds like a plan,' she said through her grin.

He laughed, pushing the hair behind her ears. 'I'd take you to bed,' he said, 'but we'd never get there in time.'

Shifting away, he pulled his wallet out of his pocket. His hands shook as he got out a small foil packet.

Her gaze dipped to the impressive ridge in his jeans.

Fascinated, she reached forward to run her fingernail down the straining denim. He grasped her wrist, though, and jerked back

'Better not,' he said, the husky tone thick with tension. 'I don't want to disappoint you.'

She wanted to tell him he couldn't possibly disappoint her. Didn't he know she adored him? But then all thoughts fled out of her head as he undid his zip and rolled on the condom. Her thighs tensed, the rush of renewed pleasure stunning her. Had she ever seen anything so magnificent?

He lifted her easily, wrapping his arm under her hips and wedging her back against the wall. 'Put your legs round my waist.'

She did as he demanded, gasping at the thick intrusion as he eased inside her. She moaned, any discomfort masked by the brutal swell of pleasure.

He grunted, then began to move—a gentle rocking of his hips that took him deeper still. She panted, distressed, as she felt herself losing control again—too fast, too hard.

Again her inexperienced body rebelled and her muscles clenched. The discomfort increased alongside the pleasure. He stilled, lodged inside her. 'What's wrong?'

'I'm sorry—I can't help it,' she said.

'It's okay,' he crooned. 'It feels incredible. But you're so tight. I don't want to hurt you.' He adjusted her weight, his hand easing between them. 'Let's try this,' he said, and his fingers probed. The lightning touch made her cry out as her muscles released in an unstoppable rush.

He grasped her hips, began to thrust again, rocking against the exposed nub and going so deep she felt overwhelmed by the stunning sensations. She heard herself sob as pure pleasure exploded along her nerve-endings and she hurtled into oblivion. Her cries matched his muffled shout as he followed her.

'Damn.' He groaned as he collapsed against her, sounding as stunned as she felt.

He let her down carefully. She wobbled as her feet touched the floor, and he gripped her arms to steady her.

'Wow.' She gave a breathy sigh, all her inhibitions lost in the intoxicating cocktail of passion and excitement frothing inside her. 'So that's what all the fuss is about.'

He lifted his head. His lips quirked in the half-light. 'You didn't know?' he asked.

She beamed at him as she pulled her dress up, watched him adjust his own clothing. She supposed she ought to feel awkward—daft, even—but the euphoria flowing through her brain made it impossible. He'd given her something she'd thought she would never have, and she was overcome by the need to tell him how much it meant to her.

'Just so you know, you're the first bloke to pass the Meg Ryan Test,' she said, flinging her arms round his neck. 'I ought to give you a medal.'

'I'll take it,' he said, his hands settling on her bottom, dragging her close. 'But what's the Meg Ryan Test?'

She drew back, giggled at his blank look. 'You know? *When Harry Met Sally*? Meg Ryan? Billy Crystal? Classic chick-flick? She fakes an orgasm in a deli. The Meg Ryan Test is when a woman doesn't have to…' She paused, the direct look he was giving her making heat surge into her cheeks. 'Because you know the male ego can be very fragile, and before I always used to…to pretend to…' She babbled to a halt. Okay, now she felt ridiculously gauche. Why had she started this conversation anyway?

'I understand.' He smiled, the crinkles round his eyes

making her heart fly into her throat. 'I'm afraid my chick-flick knowledge is sadly lacking.' He held her face in warm palms, skimmed his thumbs over her cheekbones. 'But I'm honoured you didn't need to fake your orgasms with me.' The kiss he placed on her lips was a beguiling whisper of tenderness and affection.

She pressed her forehead to his. 'You better watch out, you know,' she murmured, aware she was grinning like an idiot again. 'I'm in danger of falling madly in love with you.'

The minute she said the words she knew she'd made a mistake. He tensed, the teasing, good-humoured light dying in his eyes. He pulled her arms down from around his neck, stroked the inside of her elbow. 'Do you mind if I use your bathroom?'

She blinked, trying not to let the sudden change in tone and topic dampen her mood. How weird. For a moment there he'd looked guilty.

'Of course not,' she said. 'It's down the hallway.' She pointed the way, forcing down uneasiness. 'I'll hunt up that coffee I promised you.'

He gave her a cursory nod. 'Great.'

She stared after him as he walked away—his tall frame and broad shoulders making the narrow hallway look even pokier than usual.

Note to Louisa: never tell a guy you're falling in love with him on a first date—she grinned to herself—even when it's the truth. He'll think you're a basketcase.

She hummed a current chart hit as she freshened herself up and scoured her tiny galley kitchen for coffee. In the end she had to settle for herbal tea. He walked into the kitchen ten minutes later—looking so gorgeous she had to stifle a romantic sigh—and took the steaming cup of rosehip and ginseng tea she handed him without complaint.

She blew on her own tea, felt the pleasant little skips of her heartbeat as his gaze fixed on her face. 'We have a problem,' he said.

Her throat thickened at the serious tone.

He placed his mug gently on the counter.

'What is it?' She forced the question out. It occurred to her she'd been tumbling into love with this man all evening and she knew next to nothing about him. Was he about to tell her he had a wife and five kids?

'The condom broke.'

'Oh!' she said, relieved for a split second.

'You're on the pill, then?'

She sobered. 'Well, no—not exactly.'

'I see.'

'But it's okay. I don't think it will be a problem.'

'How so?'

She didn't think telling him about her wildly irregular periods or the fact that she hadn't had one in nearly two months would fit with the romantic mood, so she settled for, 'My period's due in the next couple of days.' Probably. 'I'm right at the end of my cycle. I won't get pregnant, I'm sure.'

'Okay. Good.' He settled back against the counter, crossed his long legs at the ankles. 'But I'd like you to contact me if there's a problem.'

'Of course,' she said, not quite able to ignore the tingle of apprehension. Why would she need to contact him if they were dating?

He picked up his mug. 'You know, Louisa, I've enjoyed myself tonight.' His eyes swept over her. 'You're beautiful, you're smart, you're sexy, and you're really very sweet.'

Sweet? Louisa gulped her tea as the feeling of rightness that had surrounded her all evening dimmed. Was she imagining things, or did that sound ever so slightly patronising?

'You're not at all what I was expecting,' he continued. 'All of which makes the confession I've got to make very hard indeed.'

Confession? Okay, she definitely didn't like the sound of that. 'What confession?'

'First things first,' he said, putting his cup down on the counter. He folded his arms across his chest. 'You don't have a clue who I am, do you?' It didn't sound like a question, but she answered it anyway.

'Of course I do,' she said, sending him a saucy smile over the lip of her cup. 'You're Luke—Jack's squash partner.' And my very own Prince Charming, she would have added, but she didn't want him to think she was a stalker. Any more declarations of undying love would have to wait until they knew each other a bit better.

To her dismay, he didn't return her smile but looked down at his feet. 'Hell. I thought as much,' he muttered.

She clenched her hands round her cup, tried to ignore the cold feeling creeping over her. Something was wrong. But what?

When his gaze met hers it was deadly serious. 'I'm Luke Devereaux, the new Lord Berwick. You featured me in your Most Eligible Bachelors list this month.'

'You're..? Oh, I see.' But she didn't see. Her cup rattled and she plopped it down, spilling red-tinted water onto the counter.

They'd only had one rather blurred paparazzi shot of him for the magazine, but now she could see the resemblance. Still her mind wouldn't quite engage.

'What a bizarre coincidence,' she said dully.

She should be overjoyed, she supposed. The man of her dreams had just turned out to be one of the most sought-after bachelors in Britain. But she didn't feel overjoyed. She felt as if she'd just walked into a room full of people stark naked. The man standing across from her wasn't the charming, gorgeous, regular guy she'd thought he was all evening any more. He was a stranger.

The assessing look he was giving her, as if he was trying to gauge her reaction, wasn't helping to calm her nerves any.

'It wasn't a coincidence,' he said, and dread settled like a block of ice in her stomach.

'It wasn't?' What exactly was he trying to say?

His eyes flicked away from her face. 'I accepted Jack's dinner invitation this evening because I wanted to meet you. I wasn't happy about your article. It's caused me a lot of trouble in the last few weeks and…' He paused, looked back. 'I had every intention of telling you so.'

She gripped the edge of the counter to stop her hands shaking. 'I don't understand.' The look of regret on his face made an icy chill rise up her neck. 'Why didn't you say anything?'

He dragged his hand through his hair. 'When you started flirting with me I thought you knew who I was. So I played along, and then, well… It got complicated.'

She held up her hand, wanting him to stop. What was he telling her? That this whole evening had been some kind of set-up?

'Why would you do that?' she said on a broken whisper. And then suddenly she knew the answer. 'You wanted to make a fool of me.'

And he'd succeeded—big-time. She'd fallen apart in his arms, told him she was falling in love with him—she'd even told him about the Meg Ryan Test. She'd given him everything she had to give and all the time he'd despised her. Tears of anguish seared her throat but she gulped them back. The rollercoaster of emotions she'd been on all evening—the excitement, the adrenalin, the anticipation of something wonderful happening—had just plunged right off the rails into a pit of anguish and uncertainty.

'It wasn't like that,' he said impatiently. He stepped towards her. She shrank back.

'What was it like, then?' she whispered. 'Correct me if I'm wrong, but it sounds as if you have a very low opinion of me, and what I do, but you seduced me anyway.'

He lifted his hands, palms up. 'You're overreacting,' he said, frustration edging the words. 'I'd forgotten all about the article by the time we got up here.'

'Well, bully for you. Is that supposed to make me feel better?'

'There's no need to be sarcastic.' His brows lowered dangerously. 'And as it happens I had a right to be annoyed. You could at least have had the courtesy to contact me and ask me if I wanted to be on your list.'

Her mouth hung open. He couldn't be serious? Was he actually implying that this whole sordid mess was her fault? 'That's beside the point and you know it. You should have told me who you were immediately.' The truth of what he'd done hit her like a punch to the gut and she wrapped her arms round her waist. 'You seduced me to get even with me, you jerk.'

'No, I didn't,' he returned. 'And anyway, I wasn't the only one doing the seducing. I didn't hear you complaining when I was stroking you to your first orgasm.'

That did it. 'You smug, patronising—' She picked up her cup and hurled the liquid at his head.

He ducked, and her Mickey Mouse mug shattered against the kitchen cabinet, spraying him with rosehip tea. 'Calm down.' He scraped his fingers through his hair, sprinkling pink droplets onto his white T-shirt.

'Get out of my flat,' she said, her voice shaking. The moment of violence had passed, leaving her feeling weak and exhausted and as shattered as her favourite mug.

How could she have been so idiotic?

'Fine—if that's the way you want it.' He marched out of the kitchen, grabbing his jacket from the floor as he strode down the hallway.

She followed him out, hurling a few choice epithets after him, but her heart wasn't in it.

As soon as the front door slammed she slumped back against the wall. The very same wall where less than ten minutes ago Luke Devereaux had brought her to an earth-shattering orgasm. Make that two earth-shattering orgasms.

Fat tears seeped out as she bit into her lip and choked down the hiccoughing cries. She couldn't hold them back for long, though. Her legs collapsed beneath her as huge, soul-drenching sobs raked her body. Her back slid down the wall and she clasped her arms tight around her shins, burying her head against her knees in a vain attempt to hide from her own stupidity.

How could she have been such a complete and utter fool? How could she have plunged headlong into love in the space of a single evening with a guy who didn't even exist? And why, now she knew what an utter fraud Luke Devereaux really was, did her heart still feel as if it were being ripped right out of her chest?

CHAPTER SEVEN

The present

'YOU insensitive, insufferable jerk.' Louisa sneered, her shoulder muscles rigid and her insides roiling with indignation and shame. She steadfastly ignored the open wound still festering underneath that she thought she'd cauterised months ago.

She'd shed enough tears over Luke Devereaux. She wasn't about to let him get to her again with his crass comments about her sex life. 'Do you seriously think that giving me an orgasm that night somehow makes up for the appalling way you treated me?'

He sent her a sideways look, then flipped on his indicator to pass a lorry. 'All I'm saying is that the sex was as good for you as it was for me, so stop pretending otherwise. And you didn't have one orgasm, as I recall, you had several. I treated you just fine,' he finished, with enough arrogance to increase her strop to fever-pitch.

Righteous anger surged up her throat. How typical of him to miss the point completely.

'Sex isn't just about mechanics, you know, Devereaux,' she snapped. 'It's about feelings. If I had known who you were, that you wanted to punish me and humiliate me, you would never have hit the jackpot at all. So you can stop slapping yourself on the back about it.'

He gave a harsh laugh. 'The sex was hardly a punishment for either of us,' he said, with enough strained patience to make her want to hit him again.

She twisted her fingers, kept them anchored in her lap.

'Things got out of hand,' he said, his voice thin with irritation. 'I know that. But you enjoyed it, so I don't see why you're still sulking.'

'You wouldn't, you complete…' She couldn't think of anything bad enough to call him.

'And if you hadn't pried into my private life in the first place, we—'

'I never pried into your private life in that article,' she interrupted him, a tiny trickle of guilt making her bristle.

She'd once blithely compromised the privacy of others. It wasn't something she was proud of. She'd learned the hard way never to cross that line again—had left the gossipy rag *London Nights* because of it. She was not about to be lectured on journalistic ethics by someone who didn't know the first thing about them.

'There was no gossip or innuendo in that piece.' She'd made sure of it. 'The Most Eligible Bachelors list is just a bit of romantic fun for our readers. The men we feature usually adore the attention. If you're paranoid, that's your problem—not mine.'

'You put me on that list without my consent,' he barked back, his fingers clenched so tight on the steering wheel his knuckles had whitened. 'You started a stampede of debutantes, paparazzi and tabloid reporters to my door when I was trying to keep a low profile. If you don't think that's disrupting my private life you're deluding yourself.'

He braked and swung the car off the M40 and onto the suburban streets of West London.

Mr Cool and Detached seemed to be in quite a snit.

'Tough,' she said, ignoring the now much more persistent prickle of guilt.

She had nothing to feel guilty about. It wasn't her fault he'd appeared out of the blue to inherit one of the largest private estates in the country. It also wasn't her fault he was handsome, rich in his own right and unattached. And it definitely wasn't her fault that after only a few months in society he already had a reputation for being elusive—evasive, even. If he didn't think that was newsworthy, he was the delusional one, not her.

And anyway, *Blush* hadn't given a single column inch of copy space to any of the rumours about his past, or how he had ended up as Berwick's heir when they weren't related. The magazine she worked for had ethics. It was not a scandal sheet. She'd worked for one before and she knew the difference.

'I'm not responsible for the behaviour of the tabloid press or the paparazzi—or your groupies.' She paused for effect. 'And that article certainly didn't give you the right to lie to me and seduce me so you could teach me a lesson.'

He swore under his breath and then, to her astonishment, braked in the middle of the tree-lined avenue, wrenched up the handbrake and clicked on the hazard lights. He turned, pinning her with his icy gaze, barely leashed temper radiating off him.

Nerves stampeded up her spine. Okay, she hadn't meant to get him quite that annoyed.

'Let's get one thing straight,' he said, the words low and dangerous. 'What happened between us was unstoppable. A force of nature. We'd been coming on to each other all evening.' His voice deepened as his eyes blazed. 'When I pulled your clothes off, when I stroked you to orgasm, it didn't have a thing to do with revenge, or punishment, or seduction, or any other damn thing except relieving the heat that had been building between us for hours. Do you really believe I was thinking about some magazine article when you were so tight, so hot around me I could feel your heart beating? When I came so hard inside you I burst the condom and got you pregnant?'

'I... I...' Louisa shut her mouth to stop the stammering. 'There's no need to be crude,' she croaked eventually, and realised she sounded like a prude.

But what else could she say? She wanted to cling on to the belief that his seduction had been a carefully calculated, coldly methodical form of revenge. The alternative—that he'd been as carried away as she had, and the magazine article had had nothing to do with it—was far too dangerous to contemplate.

She didn't want to be drawn to this man. She didn't want to be enthralled by him. And she definitely didn't want to acknowledge the uncontrollable sexual chemistry between them. She'd been defenceless and at his mercy once before—and her common sense was telling her not to risk putting herself in that situation again even if her body was screaming exactly the opposite. What did her body know anyway? It had betrayed her once before and look what had happened!

'It's not important why you made love to me,' she said, struggling to regain her composure. She folded her arms, trying to deny the scorching heat that his tirade had ignited all over again. 'The point is it was a mistake. And we're not going to repeat it.'

He shook his head, gave a huff of disbelief. The look

of incredulity on his face shattered all her illusions without him having to say a single solitary syllable.

He took off the handbrake, stabbed the hazard lights button and drove off, muttering something that sounded like, 'If you believe that, then you really are delusional.'

Louisa ignored him, too tired and frankly too distraught to debate the point. Arguing with him was like arguing with a lump of wood anyway. Frustrating and completely pointless.

She stared out the car window, barely registering the redbrick gingerbread houses of Chiswick as they whisked past. Exhaustion and confusion overtook her. Marvellous—she wasn't only tied to this dominating, overwhelming man by the baby growing in her womb, but by an elemental passion that still had the potential to flare out of control.

And she now knew he didn't care if it did. But then why would he? He had nothing to lose. His heart—if he even had one—had never been at stake.

CHAPTER EIGHT

'I'LL be back in five minutes.'

Louisa acknowledged Luke's words with a nod and let out a long breath as the car door slammed. She watched Luke walk across the garage forecourt, his purposeful stride both assured and intimidating. Louisa shivered instinctively and pressed the button on the dashboard to turn off the car's air-conditioning. She cursed quietly. She had to stop obsessing about him—and she had to stop letting that dominant aura he exuded rattle her—or she'd be a goner.

Over the last hundred miles they'd exchanged less than ten words. She'd been grateful for the respite at first. But as the powerful car ate up the miles on the motorway out of London the tense silence had begun to take on a life of its own. A hot, stifling sensation had made her skin feel tight as she became more and more aware of the man beside her. Every time Luke shifted gears, or flipped up the indicator to change lanes, she thought of those long, competent fingers stroking her to orgasm—something he'd so thoughtfully reminded her of earlier. By the time they had passed Heathrow Airport on the M4 she'd been fidgeting like a two-year-old in her seat. She'd tried to ease

the tension by switching on the radio, but then Marvin
Gaye singing 'Sexual Healing' had purred out of the car's
top-of-the-range speakers. She'd scrambled to change
channels as the legendary soul singer's honey-sweet voice
had crooned, but the damage had been done.

Luke had glanced at her, his lips curving in a deliberately provocative smile. 'Not a bad idea,' he'd murmured,
the husky tone of his voice making her pulse tick like a
time bomb waiting to explode.

Her physical discomfort had not been helped one bit by
the fact that in the last few months her bladder had shrunk
to the size of a peanut. So far they'd stopped three times for
her to use the loo. He'd been surprisingly gracious about the
frequent stops—and she had to give him points for not men-
tioning that this was another blatant sign of her pregnancy
that she'd somehow overlooked—but she was feeling less
and less conciliatory the further they got from home.

She had a lot more pressing problems at the moment
than her unruly sex drive.

What was she going to do about her job, for instance?
How was she going to break the news of her pregnancy to
her family? Her father, staunchly traditional, was certainly
going to have something to say about his first grandchild
being born out of wedlock. After spending most of her adolescence convincing Alfredo DiMarco that she could
handle her own life, it depressed her to think she was going
to have to fight that battle all over again. And then there
was her living situation. Her postage-stamp-sized flat was
going to become even pokier when the baby arrived.

But she couldn't seem to focus on any of those burning
issues—and her inability to concentrate was all Luke
Devereaux's doing.

If he hadn't brought up the events of that night again

she wouldn't be having this uncomfortable reaction to him now. And she had a sneaking suspicion he knew it. Why exactly was he whisking her off to his country pile? And why had she acquiesced so easily? She could see now this little sojourn he'd suggested had the potential for disaster. But she hadn't managed to pluck up the courage to tell him that she'd changed her mind—that she wanted him to drop her at the nearest train station—knowing it would lead to another titanic spat.

She wasn't usually one to back down from an argument, but she simply couldn't muster the energy for it. And the further they got from London, the harder it got to say anything. The thought of her own weakness irritated her.

The man deserved to be taken down a peg or two.

Even if he hadn't meant to deceive her that night—and even if she had overreacted a little to his 'confession'—that still didn't excuse his high-handed behaviour today. He was the most infuriatingly arrogant man she'd ever met, and she certainly didn't appreciate being treated like a nincompoop who couldn't take care of herself. She'd had enough of that from her father the whole time she was growing up, and she knew men like that had to be fought head-on. You absolutely could not let them see a weakness or they'd walk all over you. So why wasn't she fighting back?

Even though the sun had started to dip towards the horizon, warm air shimmered off the tarmac, making the leather interior of the car stifling in a matter of minutes. Louisa grabbed her bag and stepped out into the dusky heat. Glad to see Luke was stuck in a long queue at the service station's checkout, she walked to one of the wooden picnic tables uninvitingly situated on the grass verge. He'd be waiting a lot longer than five minutes to pay for their petrol, which would give her a chance to freshen her make-up and prepare for combat.

Unfortunately, after slicking on lipgloss, renewing her mascara and brushing her hair till it gleamed, she still felt as if she'd been route-marched through the Patagonian jungle—hot, sweaty, achy, out of sorts and mind-numbingly tired. Slipping her emergency make-up kit back into her purse, she spotted her mobile phone and remembered something else she needed to do. Well, at least she could set some wheels in motion while she waited for battle to commence.

She needed to start getting her life back on track. She'd had a huge shock today, but that was no excuse to start panicking—or, worse yet, go into denial. She'd done quite enough of that already over the last few months.

There was only one person she would trust to advise her. Her best friend Mel Devlin. She should have told Mel about her night with Devereaux months ago. That Mel had noticed the consequences before Louisa herself only went to prove how intuitive her best friend was.

She dialled Mel's number.

Her spirits deflated when she heard Mel and Jack's answering machine message.

'Hi, Mel, it's me—Louisa. I really need to talk to you. I've got…' She hesitated. She couldn't tell Mel about Devereaux or the baby in an answer-machine message. 'I've got some news. Some big news. I'll ring back later.'

She ended the call and then dialled her GP's surgery in Camden. There was one other thing she wanted to get sorted right away. She didn't want her antenatal care in the hands of the good Dr Lester. She couldn't afford a Harley Street doctor, and she didn't want Devereaux paying the woman's no-doubt exorbitant fees. Especially as she wasn't even sure what his intentions were towards the baby.

She watched the service station's entrance as she waited for her call to go through. She couldn't see the checkout queue from this angle, but there was still no sign of Devereaux. She turned to sit down, propping her back against the table and staring at the cars zipping by on the A303. The surgery's answer-machine message finally clicked in on the tenth ring.

For goodness' sake, what was this? Avoid Louisa day?

'Hi, this is Louisa DiMarco. I'd like to make an appointment with Dr Khan at the earliest possible opportunity. I'll make sure I attend. Please call me back—'

'What the hell are you doing?'

Louisa yelped, dropped the phone, and spun round to see Devereaux towering over her.

'Are you mad?' Her hands were shaking. 'You scared the life out of me!'

'What's the appointment for?' he demanded, taking her arm and hauling her off the picnic bench.

'Why are you listening in on my telephone conversations?' she snapped back as she slapped her palm against his chest. It was hard as rock.

Her courage deserted her when she saw the icy rage on his face. She scrambled back, but the picnic table prodding her hips stopped her retreat. What was wrong with him?

He dragged her back.

'You're not aborting the child,' he said, his voice low with suppressed fury. 'I won't allow it.'

She should have demanded he let her go. Should have told him the decision to have the baby was her choice, not his. But she was so shocked by the force of his anger, and the raw, turbulent emotion swirling in his eyes, she simply blurted out, 'I'm not having an abortion. I couldn't.'

His eyes narrowed, the fury still bubbling. 'You're lying. I heard you make an appointment.'

'No, you didn't.' She struggled against his iron grip, realised she was stuck fast. 'I was making an appointment with my GP to sort out my antenatal care.'

'Why?' he said, loosening his fingers at last. 'It's already been arranged.'

'Not by me it hasn't.' She tugged her arm out of his grasp, rubbed the skin where his fingers had dug in, and felt her own temper ignite. What was she playing at? She shouldn't be on the defensive here. He had no right to talk to her like this. To manhandle her.

'I want my own GP treating me during my pregnancy. Not that it's any of your business,' she said firmly.

'Don't be ridiculous. Lester's one of the top obstetricians in the country.' That raw, savage fury had disappeared, to be replaced by the condescending proprietorial tone she hated.

Her fighting spirit kicked in with a vengeance.

'I don't care if Lester's the top obstetrician in the known universe. It's my decision who provides my antenatal care, just as it's my decision whether or not I have this baby. Not yours,' she shouted, her chest heaving with all the force and fury of a heroine in a penny-dreadful novel. How dared he presume to tell her what she was and wasn't allowed to do with her own body? 'Because, in case it's escaped your notice, *I'm* the one having this baby. Not you.'

He frowned, but didn't look all that chastened. 'Considering the great job you've been doing so far, you ought to be grateful for my involvement,' he said. 'After all, if it wasn't for me you wouldn't even know there *was* a baby,' he finished, but at a considerably reduced volume.

He sounded ever so slightly less sure of himself.

Louisa took heart. 'Well, now I do know. So I can take things from here.' She bent to pick up her phone, shoved it back in her bag. 'I want you to drop me at the nearest train station. I've decided I'm going back to London.' She swung the strap of her bag over her shoulder. 'And from now on you can keep your great big interfering nose out of my affairs.'

She was feeling pretty good about her parting shot—until she went to march past him. He gripped her hips and stepped into her path, stopping her dead as she bumped into him.

'Not so fast,' he said, the volume now at a dangerously low level.

She struggled, bringing her hands up to his chest, but he just wrapped his arms around her and held her still. 'What are you doing?' she asked, her voice breaking on an annoyingly feeble squeak.

'You're not going anywhere until we get a few things straight.'

'There's nothing to get straight,' she said, still squeaking. He was so close she could see the flecks of blue in his irises, and her belly was pressed against something that was fast becoming even less accommodating.

She quivered, felt the treacherous response at her core and hated herself.

'I'm the father of this baby,' he said softly, but there was no mistaking the menace in his tone. 'Which means I get a say in every single detail of its life. So you'd better get used to the idea. I don't shirk my responsibilities and I'm not shirking this one.'

The implication that she had shirked her responsibilities up till today was clear, and Louisa felt a dart of shame pierce her armour. He'd scored a hit, and she could see he knew it when his lips curved in a confident grin.

'And it's a good thing you don't want an abortion—because if you did you would have a major fight on your hands. No one hurts what's mine.'

On some subconscious level she supposed she ought to be grateful that he was so determined to defend their child, but Louisa couldn't get past her fury at his macho self-righteousness. The same helpless anger had dogged her throughout her adolescence—had forced her to rebel whenever her father had insisted she do what he said, whether she liked it or not.

If Luke Devereaux thought he could decide what was best for her and her baby just because he was the father he could think again. And she didn't like the way he was talking about the baby as if he owned it.

'I don't take orders from you, Devereaux,' she said, between pants as she tried to wrestle out of his embrace. 'Not now and not ever. And we happen to be talking about a child here. Not your personal possession.'

She braced her hands against his chest and shoved. He didn't budge an inch.

She struggled some more, then heaved out a breath and gave up, well aware of the satisfied look on his face. Her struggles were futile. They were only tiring her out and increasing the friction between them. She could feel him more prominently now than ever, against her belly.

She should have been outraged by his blatant arousal, but her own hormones weren't exactly indifferent to him either—in fact they were having a little party of their own. She glared at him.

'Stop being such a bully,' she said. 'We both know you're stronger than I am—but in this day and age it doesn't make you right. You can let me go now, because the Neanderthal routine's getting tiresome,' she finished, trying to sound bored despite the quiver in her voice.

'I'll let you go when you promise to listen to what I have to say.'

'Fine—say your piece, Mr Caveman,' she said, angry all over again that he was using his physical strength—and her inevitable response—against her. 'But that doesn't mean I'm going to do what you say.'

He loosened his grip, but not enough to allow her to step away. She could still smell him—and the tantalising bulge in his trousers wasn't getting any smaller.

'Let me go. You promised,' she said, suddenly desperate to put some distance between them and the heat that was building. They'd never get anything settled at this rate—and she wasn't about to let him ravish her in a petrol station, whatever her traitorous hormones might want.

'Stay there—and stop acting the innocent.' He barked out the words.

But she could hear the strain in his voice, could see the small beads of sweat forming on his brow, and then she heard a shuffling noise to her right. She glanced round and realised exactly why he was so eager to keep her close. She turned back to him, a sly smile on her lips.

The balance of power had finally shifted in her favour.

It was the Friday evening before a Bank Holiday weekend, and the service station was crowded with holidaymakers—any one of whom would be able to witness Devereaux's aroused state if she stepped back.

Despite the fact that her own libido was on full alert, Louisa enjoyed a sharp spurt of satisfaction at Devereaux's predicament. Having three older brothers, it simply wasn't in Louisa's nature to let the moment pass without going in for the kill. She moved closer and swivelled her hips, brushing herself against his erection, and heard him curse softly. She edged her palms up his chest, slid her fingers under the collar of his shirt. His broad shoulders tensed and he shuddered.

'What the hell are you doing?' he muttered.

She caressed the damp skin of his neck, ran her fingers through the short curls at his nape, inhaled the pleasantly musky smell of his sweat—and savoured the sharp scent of victory. He was having a really tough time with this. She welcomed the quick thrill as she traced her nail across his cheek, pressed the pad of her index finger against his bottom lip and felt his now massive erection buck through their clothing.

She had him now. 'I'm showing you who's boss, big boy,' she purred.

She saw the flash of challenge in his eyes, and knew that she'd just made a potentially catastrophic tactical error.

She dropped her arms, jerked away. But he dragged her back. He ground his hardness against the juncture of her thighs, bent over her and bit into the sensitive cord in her neck. She stifled a scream as molten heat blasted up from her core.

'Don't—there are people around,' she choked, her hands trembling as she pushed against him. The burning between her thighs was so intense now she thought she might collapse. She didn't want to play any more. She should have guessed he wouldn't play fair.

She struggled, but he held her fast and whispered in her ear. 'You started this, and when we get to Havensmere I intend to finish it. But until then you'll do as you're told, or we're going to be stuck here all night.'

'I'm not going to Havensmere. I told you that. And

anyway, you can't keep it up all night. It's not physically possible, is it?'

He drew back enough to give her a damning look. 'I got hard just thinking about you for nearly a week after we made love that night, so where you're concerned take my word for it. Anything's possible.'

She ignored the reckless thrill at his words. So she turned him on? It was nothing to be proud of.

He shifted, holding her at a distance, but made sure her body masked his from the crowds passing by. 'Put your hands on my hips,' he said, his voice more strained than ever. 'But don't try any funny business or you'll pay later. I guarantee it.'

His tense threat made her realise the ridiculousness of their situation. A giggle popped out of her mouth before she could stop it.

'Laugh all you want,' Luke said sternly, but his lips quirked, and his eyes sparkled with humour. 'We'll see who's laughing when I'm so deep inside you tonight you can hardly breathe.'

She swallowed, not finding the situation all that funny any more. 'I'm not going to Havensmere tonight. I told you I've changed my mind. I'm going back to London.'

His eyebrows lifted, but he looked curious rather than annoyed. 'Louisa, sweetheart,' he said heavily, giving a long-suffering sigh, 'we've already had this fight—remember? If we start replaying the ones we've already had, it'll take us for ever to get to the important ones.' He smiled at her, the soft, sensual curve of his lips making her stomach sink. 'The baby's going to be here in six months—time is limited.'

She couldn't help it. She smiled back. She'd completely forgotten about his dry sense of humour and that heart-melting smile—both dangerously sexy and boyishly charming, with a brooding quality that had made her want to coax it out of him every chance she got. In a flash of insight she understood why he'd captivated her that night. It hadn't been his movie-star looks, the perfect manners, that to-die-for physique, or even his skill as a lover. It had been that raw magnetism and his ability to make her laugh.

The thought of how heavily she'd fallen for him made her sober. Her eyes drifted down to his chest. She concentrated on the wisps of chest hair she could see above the open collar of his shirt, tried to think sensibly.

It was hardly surprising she'd forgotten the man she'd met that night. He didn't exist—not really. Maybe he could still be funny and charming when he wanted to be—and it was obvious the sexual attraction between them was as potent as ever—but today had proved they had very little in common except this baby. She couldn't afford to lose sight of that.

He hooked a finger under her chin, drew her eyes to his. 'Why have you changed your mind about coming to Havensmere?'

'You know very well why,' she said. What was the point in being coy? 'The sex thing is going to get in the way if we're alone together. It already has and we're not even alone yet.'

He stroked her hips, his eyes dark and amused. 'I'm glad to hear you finally admit that. But I don't see why it's a problem.'

'You wouldn't,' she said, feeling exasperated. Why did he have to be so irresistible while she was trying to be sensible? 'Your life hasn't been turned upside down today and—'

'Of course it has,' he interrupted her. 'In case you didn't realise, I hadn't planned on becoming a father. Certainly not like this.'

She placed her hands on his forearms, sent him a weary smile. 'Please, let's not argue again. I've had about as much conflict as I can take for today.' She knew it sounded lame, but she'd been on an emotional rollercoaster the whole day and she suddenly felt overwhelmed.

Tears welled in her eyes and she gulped them back.

'Hey, don't cry. It's not that bad.' He brushed his thumb across her lower lip and kissed her forehead gently. The tears coursed down her cheeks.

'I have to go home—start sorting my life out. There's so much to do,' she said, choking back a sob.

She knew it was foolish—and hopelessly self-indulgent—but she couldn't seem to stop the flood of tears. The enormity of everything that had happened today seemed to be closing in on her, pressing down on her chest until she couldn't breathe.

He placed his arm round her shoulder and pulled a hankie out of his back pocket. 'Don't worry. We'll work it out,' he said, handing her a monogrammed square of clean white cotton.

She buried her nose in it, recognised the detergent smell from that moment in the ultrasound suite when he'd wiped away her tears earlier that day, and started to sob.

He turned her towards him and folded her into his arms. Firm hands stroked her back as he murmured reassurances in her ear. Although she knew the comfort he offered was only temporary she gave herself up to it and let the tears out. Eventually the crying began to pass. She blew her nose hard, scrubbed the hankie over her cheeks, feeling embarrassed at her mini-breakdown.

He dipped his head to peer into her face. 'All finished?'

The concerned frown almost had her starting all over again.

She gulped back another little hiccough. 'I'm fine. It must be the pregnancy hormones. They make me feel as if I'm trapped in a bad TV soap opera.' She sniffed again, wiped under her eyes to try and repair the damage. His monogrammed handkerchief was a sodden mess when she'd finished, and stained with her mascara. She probably had the worst panda eyes in history, she thought, but was too tired to care.

'Sorry,' she said, offering him the hankie. 'I've ruined it.'

'Keep it,' he said, steering her towards his car. 'I've got others.' He opened the door, ushered her inside.

She waited until he'd settled in the driver's seat before she spoke. 'I know I've put you to a lot of trouble today, but if you could drop me at the nearest train station I'd be eternally grateful. If you give me your phone number, I'll call you in the next couple of weeks. We can talk then about…' She paused. 'You know…' What, exactly?

Future scans? Antenatal classes? Baby names, for goodness' sake? How involved did he really intend to be? And how involved did she want him to be? She gave a jerky sigh, stared down at his scrunched-up hankie in her fist. She felt as if she was climbing Mount Everest and didn't have any of the right equipment. If only she knew him better she might know where to start.

'You know…baby stuff,' she said finally, feeling like a complete twit.

He studied her, his expression unreadable.

Please don't make an issue of this now, she thought desperately. I've got too much to cope with already.

Eventually he nodded and said, 'Right—baby stuff.'

She let out the breath she'd been holding, her relief immense. If he'd pressed his advantage she might well have given in to him—which would definitely have been bad. She needed time and space to sort herself and her life out before she confronted the whole thorny issue of how to deal with Luke Devereaux. But one thing she did know. Letting him make her decisions for her was not an option.

He leaned into the back seat and gripped his jacket, handed it to her. 'Why don't you fold that up and use it as a pillow? You can have a nap before we get there. You look shattered.'

Her bottom lip quivered at his thoughtfulness. She bit into it. Get a grip, woman.

'Thanks,' she said, successfully stifling another sob. She glanced at the dark blue jacket draped across her lap— and gasped.

His head whipped round. 'What's the matter?'

'I can't use this as a pillow,' she said, horrified. 'It'll crease dreadfully, and anyway it's new season Armani. It'd be practically sacrilegious.'

His face relaxed and he chuckled. He shifted into gear and put his arm across the back of her seat. 'I promise I won't tell Armani if you don't,' he said, winking at her as he glanced round to reverse out of the space.

She smiled and nodded, trying to ignore the flutter in her belly at the glint of mischief in his eyes. But she couldn't ignore the wistfulness that settled over her as her cheek pressed against the folded linen.

It smelled of him—citrus and musk, masculine and exclusive. Delicious and dangerous. Just like its owner, she thought, as she drifted into an exhausted sleep.

CHAPTER NINE

LUKE watched the wrought-iron gates of Havensmere swing open, waved to old Joe the lodge keeper, and eased the vehicle over the cattle grid. He could hear the clanking mechanism close behind the car as he purred up the long, winding drive. The summer evening settled around him. With the soft top down, he could hear the rustle of leaves as the drive's ancient chestnut trees shifted in the sluggish breeze, mottling the car's paintwork in comforting shadows.

After five minutes the house came into view round the final bend, its Palladian splendour nestled against the chalk downs. Twin staircases climbed in facing semicircles to the first floor. Stone pillars topped by a pair of lions that looked more bored than predatory flanked the double-doored entrance.

He noticed the gardening team had added the dark blue lobelia he'd suggested to the raised flowerbeds skirting the drive. The final job of repairing the plasterwork and sand-blasting the frontage was scheduled to begin next month—not a moment too soon, he thought as he stared at the crumbling cornice on the second storey.

He tapped his thumb on the steering wheel, his reaction to the house as confused as always. When he'd first seen the place twenty-three years ago he'd been both spellbound by its beauty and intimidated by its grandeur. To a child who'd spent the first seven years of his life in a two-room apartment on the wrong end of the Las Vegas strip, Havensmere had seemed magnificent and terrifying—the cold, unforgiving stone magnifying both his grief and his loneliness. And once he'd been ushered into Berwick's study the miserable feeling of abandonment had only increased. The man sitting behind the desk had been as contemptuous as his house.

When he'd been summoned back here a year ago, for the reading of Berwick's will, those old resentments had burned inside him—until he'd seen Havensmere again. With its neglected plasterwork, dried-up flowerbeds and potholed driveway, it hadn't been the sentinel of remembered pain he had been expecting, but rather a sad, forlorn and mocking reminder of past glories. In the end he supposed it was pity that had persuaded him to pay for the extensive restorations from his own pocket—but once the work was finished he intended to return to his Chelsea penthouse.

What exactly he was going to do with the place when he left, he had no idea.

He sighed and looked at his passenger, curled up in her seat. With the engine turned off he could hear the steady murmur of her breathing. One thing was for sure: he had a much bigger problem now than Havensmere, and it was sleeping soundly next to him, looking as innocent as a child.

Louisa DiMarco—mother of his unborn baby, artless seductress, and all-round pain in the backside. There was going to be hell to pay tomorrow morning when she woke up and found out where she was.

He smiled. Despite the fireworks to come, he didn't have a single regret about his decision to bring her to

Havensmere once she'd fallen asleep. He'd meant what he'd said about taking his responsibilities seriously. And she was his responsibility now—whether she liked it or not.

Her eyelashes fluttered and she moaned, snuggling into his jacket, but her breathing remained deep and even. She had to be utterly exhausted to sleep so soundly in what looked like a very uncomfortable position. His gaze drifted down her frame. As he stared at the gentle rise and fall of her breasts beneath skin-tight cotton he remembered the feel of her, soft and fragrant, pressed against him at the service station. He felt himself stir and was forced to admit that the baby wasn't the main reason he'd brought Louisa to the secluded country estate.

Every damn thing about the woman turned him on. She had the full, voluptuous figure of an Italian love goddess on the long, leggy frame of an athlete. Her sultry scent and those dark almond-shaped eyes only added to the package, promising sexual secrets that no man could resist uncovering.

He knew Louisa would never be his ideal mate. She was far too volatile and impetuous for that. He pulled his keys out of the ignition and his lips curved—but as a short-term playmate she had definite potential.

After ten years of building a multimillion-pound business empire he'd got into the habit of telling people to jump and then waiting for them to ask how high. Maybe it was the novelty of having someone do exactly the opposite that he found so appealing, so tantalising about her. He thrived on challenges, and he'd never had any woman challenge him the way she did. Eventually the novelty would wear off, but until that happened why not enjoy the fireworks?

He shoved his car keys into his pocket and got out of the car. As he had suspected, Louisa barely stirred as he lifted her into his arms and carried her up the front steps. His footman, Albert, held the sturdy oak door open and gave Luke a friendly nod as he strolled past.

Luke hefted his guest and took the sweeping staircase to the first floor. She was surprisingly light for a woman of her height. It occurred to him she wouldn't stay that way for too much longer. The picture of her svelte figure swollen with his child made him feel a little uneasy—he didn't want to think that far ahead—but it also filled him with an odd feeling of possessiveness and pride.

She sighed then, the soft breath feathering his neck. He took several calming breaths as the blood surged into his groin. By the time he got to the Rose Room, the suite his housekeeper had prepared for Louisa, he was relieved to discover the ever-efficient Mrs Roberts had turned down the bed. He placed Louisa carefully on the king-sized four-poster. She rolled over and drew her knees up, tucking her hands under her head.

His erection mercifully began to subside.

He took his time unzipping her boots and sliding them down her well-toned calves, then tucked her footwear under his arm. He'd keep these with him for now—in case she got any wild ideas about running off in the middle of the night.

He draped the quilted coverlet over her, and noticed the way her full breasts plumped up against the plunging neckline of her frock. She wouldn't be all that comfortable in the morning, when she awoke in her clothes. But no way was he going to help her out of them. There was a limit to how noble he could be.

He tugged the drapes closed on the large bay windows, shutting out the evening sunlight. On his way out of the room he stopped for a moment by the bed and studied her in the darkness.

He touched her hair, taking advantage of the calm before the storm, and ran his fingers over the soft, silky curls.

Maybe he was losing his mind, but he was already looking forward to tomorrow's confrontation. She might want to fight him, but he was confident her passionate nature would be her undoing—and then they'd both get to enjoy her surrender.

CHAPTER TEN

LOUISA inhaled the luxurious scent of clean linen and the hint of roses as her eyelids fluttered open. Rich red velvet drapes hung about a foot from her nose, their sashes woven with gold thread that glinted in a thin sliver of sunlight. She blinked, but the opulent, unfamiliar decor was still there.

She rubbed her eyes, tried again, and took in the canopy above her head, hung with the same heavy velvet, and the ornate posts made of carved mahogany.

What on earth was she doing in a four-poster bed?

She pushed up onto her elbows and scanned the strange room in the half-light. It was enormous, at least twice the size of her whole flat, and the large pieces of matching antique furniture—a dressing table, a wardrobe, a table with upholstered chairs—did nothing to diminish the lavish feeling of space. Ten-foot-high bay windows across the room were shielded with the same maroon velvet curtains as the bed, cutting out all but a few shards of sunlight.

How peculiar. She'd never had a dream set in Scarlett O'Hara's boudoir before.

But then her eyes settled on her hideously wrinkled dress—and a string of images from the day before blasted into her mind like a movie on fast-forward.

Luke's steely grey eyes, flat and furious, as he leaned over her desk; the three-dimensional picture of their baby flickering on the ultrasound screen; Luke's long fingers gripping the steering wheel of his car; the feel of him, hard and ready, outlined against her abdomen at the dusty service station.

Twin tides of outrage and arousal surged through her.

She flung back the satin quilt, scrambled off the bed and shot across the room, her bare feet sinking into a silk rug. She whipped back the velvet drapes and flinched as a burst of sunlight dazzled her. Then gaped as the landscape framed by mullioned glass came into focus.

The South Downs rose in the distance, dwarfing ancient woodlands which skirted over an acre of manicured lawn. She pushed up on tiptoe and peered down to see formal gardens surrounding the house, their beds bursting with summer blooms.

This wasn't a dream. It was a nightmare.

That infuriating man had only gone and kidnapped her again!

Louisa rolled up the sleeves of the silk robe she'd found folded on a shelf under the vanity unit, finger-combed her hair and assessed her appearance in the bathroom mirror. She looked impossibly young and vulnerable in the over-sized robe. Not the image she wanted to convey to Devereaux at all. But her shower had refreshed her, and at least she'd had a good night's sleep. Now all she had to do was get her clothes and her make-up on and she would be ready to face Luke Devereaux—the rat.

Of all the miserable, dishonest, low-down, sneaky tricks. When she went downstairs she was going to give her kidnapper a really good piece of her mind about his latest crime before she sailed past him out the door. She hadn't quite dealt with how she was going to get home, with no shoes, no car and no money, but she'd figure something out. The point was, she was not going to be treated like this.

But as Louisa stepped out of the bathroom in her robe—and was blinded by the sunshine streaming through the now open drapes—she realised Devereaux, as per usual, had his own agenda.

'Hello, Louisa.' The deep, intimate rumble of his voice brought an infuriating shiver of awareness.

Louisa flung an arm up to shield her eyes and glared. He looked relaxed and in control, lounging in an armchair by the table, wearing a pair of faded jeans and a pale blue polo shirt. The casual attire threw her for a moment—reminding her of how he'd looked on their first night together—but then she spotted her boots by his feet.

'What are you doing in my room?' she managed on a croak of outrage.

'It's nearly one o'clock.' He stood up and walked towards her. 'Lunch is ready. I thought we could eat on the terrace.'

She stepped back, then curled her bare toes into the carpet and forced herself to stand her ground. Her chin rose as he stopped in front of her.

At five foot seven, and being a firm believer that anything lower than a four-inch heel was for gym wear only, Louisa rarely had to look up to meet a man's gaze. Even with only his loafers on Luke Devereaux was over half a foot taller than her.

It was one more black mark against him.

'I have absolutely no intention of eating lunch with you,' she snapped. 'As soon as I'm dressed I'm leaving.'

His lips twisted in a sardonic smile. A hot flush worked its way up her neck as he scanned her figure. How had he got the upper hand again? Without a stitch of clothing on under the flimsy silk, and not a dot of make-up on either, she might as well have been stark naked. What she wouldn't do right now for a smidgen of lipgloss.

'Think again,' he said. His gaze flicked down to her midriff. 'You need to eat something—especially in your condition. And you're not going anywhere until you do.'

That did it. The curt, dismissive statement had Louisa's temper shooting straight from smouldering embers to raging inferno. 'You can't stop me,' she announced as she charged past him and stomped round the four-poster bed— which now looked obscenely large. She flung open the door to the suite. 'Now, get out of my room.'

He crossed his arms over his chest, propped his shoulder against one of the bedposts and lifted one dark brow. But made absolutely no move to obey her command.

'As much as I enjoy your little tantrums, Louisa,' he said, in that patronising tone he had to know by now drove her insane, 'I'm getting hungry myself. So why don't you stop behaving like a petulant child and come down to lunch so we can discuss this like adults?'

She gasped, her hand dropping off the door handle. The unbelievable cheek of the man. Sorry—*rat*.

'I'm not the child here. You are.'

She'd slapped her hands on her hips, ready to give him both barrels, when his gaze dipped to her bosom. She glanced down and her tongue stalled as she realised he could see right down her cleavage. She grappled to pull her lapels together, her nipples tightening painfully, the smooth silk feeling like sandpaper under that assessing gaze.

His lips twitched as his eyes finally lifted back to her

face. 'You were saying?' he enquired, as if they'd been talking about the weather.

She cleared her throat, crossed her arms over her chest and tried to get a hold on her indignation. 'I'm not going to sit down and have lunch with you after you kidnapped me.'

He huffed out an incredulous laugh. 'Don't you think you're overreacting?'

'No, I don't,' she shouted. She stopped to drag a deep breath into her lungs. She mustn't start screaming like a banshee. Hysteria now would only stoke that superiority complex of his. 'No, I don't,' she repeated, as calmly as she could manage. 'You said you'd take me to the nearest railway station and you lied.'

'I never said any such thing,' he replied with infuriating certainty.

She scoured her mind, trying to remember what he had or hadn't said, and then realised he had deliberately side-tracked her. 'I don't care what you said,' she sputtered. 'You knew I didn't want to come to Havensmere so you shouldn't have brought me here. It's as simple as that.'

'Not quite,' he said, pushing himself upright.

She found herself backing up again as he stepped forward, that languid grace more predatory than ever. 'Don't come any closer,' she said, thrusting her palm up, brutally aware of what she didn't have on under her robe.

He kept coming, forcing her to retreat as her hand touched soft cotton—and felt the tensile strength beneath.

'You were exhausted, emotional, and probably suffering from shock—and you're pregnant with my child,' he said, layering on the condescension. He touched her cheek, the tenderness in his eyes disconcerting her. 'You don't seriously think I was going to put you on a train in that condition?'

She jerked her head away, but too late. The tingling

warmth was already spreading like wildfire. 'Do you mind? You're invading my personal space,' she said, trying for flippant but getting breathless instead.

He framed her face in his palms, that megawatt smile sending heat blazing through her. 'That's the general idea,' he said, his breath stirring her hair as he angled his head. 'Your eyes go black when you're aroused, you know,' he murmured. 'It's a dead giveaway—along with those nipples.'

She grasped his upper arms, tried to hold him back with shaking hands, but her insides were already molten with need. 'This isn't going to settle anything. I'm still furious with you—and I still want to go home,' she said. But the quiver in her voice meant the words sounded more like an invitation than a rebuke.

'We'll argue about it later,' he whispered, thrusting his fingers into her hair, his thumbs caressing the line of her jaw. 'Right now I want to invade more of your personal space.'

And then his lips slanted across hers.

She braced herself, tried to ignore the flood of longing. But the kiss went from harsh to coaxing in a heartbeat. His tongue swept inside, sending shockwaves through her system as if she'd been plugged into an electric socket. Her fingers flexed in the soft cotton of his shirt and, entirely of its own accord, her tongue delved back, duelling with his in a sensual battle she knew she couldn't win.

She'd put him in his place in a minute, she thought dimly. As soon as she regained the power of speech. Right now all that mattered was letting those demanding lips feast on hers.

His chest flattened her breasts, rubbing hard against engorged nipples, and she heard the gentle thud as her back hit the wall. He devoured her neck, sucked on the pulse-point, and hot lava surged upwards.

Her head fell back as his rough palm cruised up her thigh under the whisper of silk. She groaned. 'We can't do this. We don't have time,' she murmured, feeling the last of her sanity being swept away on a sea of sensation.

His thumb skimmed the sensitive skin at the top of her thigh. He lifted her leg, hooked it over his hip, exposing her melting core to the hard ridge in his jeans as he pressed it against her.

'We've got a week—I've already arranged it with Parker,' he muttered.

She moaned and pushed against him, the unyielding hardness incredible through the thin covering of silk and denim.

But then his harsh whisper replayed in her brain and the words registered.

Her eyes shot open. 'You did what?' she shouted, shoving him away. She teetered precariously as sanity slammed back into her like a bucket of ice water.

'What's the matter?' he growled, his eyes stormy with passion and his breathing as ragged as her own.

'You arranged a week's leave for me with my boss?' She couldn't believe it.

'Yes. So what?' He sounded confused.

'So what? So you had no right, that's what.'

He grasped her wrist, dragged her back into his arms. 'Forget it. We're not arguing about this now.'

'Yes, we are.' She slammed her hands into his chest and twisted her head as he tried to kiss her. 'Stop it.' She wriggled some more. 'We're not doing this now.'

'But we're both about to explode,' he cried.

You don't say, she thought, the heat still pumping

through her and making her knees wobbly. 'I don't care. I want to know why you spoke to my boss.'

'Oh, for…' He swore viciously and let her go. 'Your timing stinks, you know that?' he said, glaring at her with enough aroused fury to melt steel. 'All right—fine.' He dragged his fingers through his hair, making the carefully styled waves furrow into uneven rows. 'Let's get this out of the way.'

'Yes, let's,' she said, crossing her arms over her now heaving chest.

'We're not going to get anything sorted in a single day,' he shot at her, not sounding remotely conciliatory, 'so I phoned Parker at home last night to arrange more time. What the hell is wrong with that?'

'What's *wrong* with that?' She gawped at him. Was he serious? 'Maybe you should take a wild guess.'

'I can't guess. I have no idea what the problem is.'

The red haze cleared slightly. He was looking at her as if she'd gone completely mad.

'You really don't get it, do you?' she asked.

'Get what?' He bit the words off, clearly as annoyed and frustrated as she was.

The last of the anger, the outrage, drained out of her, to be replaced by a numb feeling of unreality. How could anyone be so totally clueless about personal boundaries?

'You don't get to arrange my leave for me. *I* do that,' she said, not quite able to believe she was having to explain this to him. 'Just like you don't get to decide whether or not I come to Havensmere. That's my decision, not yours. You're worse than my father.'

'But it was the right decision,' he said, as if that fact were remotely relevant. 'A week at Havensmere will do you good. You need to get your strength back.' He stepped closer—close enough for her to see the determination in his eyes. 'And then there's the sex—after what's just happened I'm thinking one day isn't going to be long enough to work that out of our systems either.'

'We're not having sex.'

'Why the hell not?'

'Because I say so,' she hurled back. He was getting pushy again, and she wasn't going to stand for it. 'I told you, sex will only get in the way.'

He cursed. 'All the more reason to get it out of the way, then. We've been apart for three months and the attraction is still there, as strong as ever. If you think we're going to be able to ignore it, you're nuts.'

He might have a point about that, she thought, her sex still throbbing, clamouring for the release she knew only he could give her. But she wasn't about to admit it. He wasn't going to use sex as yet another weapon in the power struggle between them.

If they made love again it was going to be on her terms, not his.

'We're not getting anything out of the way until you stop treating me like you own me. I want you to apologise for your high-handed behaviour, and I want you to promise not to make any more choices for me again, or I'm walking out right now.'

'For heaven's sake, I was looking after you—and I'm not apologising for it.'

Louisa forced down the traitorous spurt of warmth. So what if he'd been trying to help her? It didn't give him the right to ride roughshod over her wishes whenever it suited him.

'I mean it, Luke. I'm not eating lunch with you until you

promise me you won't do this again. I'm not a child and I won't be treated like one.'

'You're mad!' he shouted.

He looked bigger than ever. She didn't care.

'You haven't eaten since yesterday afternoon and you're prepared to starve yourself to make a stupid point?' he said, frustration pulsing off him.

'Missing a meal won't kill me,' she said. 'If the Suffragettes could do it, so can I.'

'What are you talking about?'

'The Suffragettes,' she said calmly, even though her insides were churning at the thought of what was really at stake here. 'Those pesky females who fought for women's rights.' If they were ever going to have a chance of dealing with this baby together she had to win this round.

'I know who the Suffragettes are,' he grunted, then spun away and paced across the room. His stiff, angry strides lacked his usual grace.

He braced his hands on his hips as he stared out the window. His shoulders looked like carved rock silhouetted against the sunshine. Clearly he'd never had an ultimatum like this before, and he didn't have a clue how to deal with it. Well, good—it was about time he learned that not every female on the planet was prepared to bow to his every whim.

The expertly mown lawn dissolved in an angry haze in front of Luke's eyes. He was so annoyed with Louisa he wanted to throttle her. The woman was turning out to be more of a challenge than he'd anticipated—and not the enjoyable kind.

Onc minute they'd been about to devour each other, and the next she'd been talking a load of rubbish about

rights and decisions and demanding he apologise for…
For what, exactly? He didn't even know what he'd done
that was so terrible.

To add injury to insult, he was so hard in his jeans it was
a wonder he hadn't made a complete fool of himself.

Nobody told him what to do—especially not someone
who'd been so vulnerable the night before that he'd had to
mop up her tears and tuck her into bed like a baby. She
needed him to take care of her. If she'd just admit that they
could get past all this nonsense and get back to what
mattered. And right now relieving the ache in his groin was
top of the list.

But how had she turned the tables on him so neatly?
She'd been as ready as he had a moment ago. He'd heard
that staggered moan, smelt the intoxicating scent of her
arousal. But she'd still managed to pull back. He knew she
could be stubborn, and over-emotional, and contrary, but
where had this backbone of steel come from?

He rubbed the back of his neck, tried to focus on the
problem.

What mattered in any negotiation was the bottom line.
And the bottom line here was that he wanted Louisa to
stay—for a week at the very least. So they could finish
what they'd started—both in bed and out. It was pretty
obvious she had a problem with any kind of authority—
so he'd have to tread more carefully.

He turned around. She was watching him, waiting, her
eyes flinty with determination, her fingers clasped tight on
the lapels of her robe. She looked valiant, despite the bare
feet and freshly scrubbed face—like a warrior instead of
the fanciful, inexperienced girl he'd once taken her for.
Why he found that attractive, he had no idea.

As he approached her he noticed how her puckered

nipples stood proud against the thin fabric of the robe. She was no more immune to him than he was to her—he might have to concede this battle but he would still win the war.

Louisa could see he'd calmed down, but her stomach muscles were still taut with nerves. If he didn't apologise now she would have to leave—and in the last few minutes she'd realised she didn't want to. Not yet.

Although she wasn't really sure why.

They'd spent nearly the whole of the last twenty-four hours bickering. And when they weren't bickering…Well, the overpowering desire to get naked with him didn't make their association seem any more promising, really. But as she took in his tall, elegant frame, that devastating face, the thick hair falling in careless waves across his brow and the carefully hooded eyes, she realised she found Luke Devereaux as intriguing as he was infuriating.

The man was an enigma—and a devastatingly sexy one at that. And she wanted to know a lot more about him. Who was he? What made him tick? And why did he captivate her, even though he appeared to have the sensitivity of a gnat?

But first they'd have to get his ego under strict supervision.

He buried his hands in the back pockets of his jeans. The stance made him look a little wary. She considered it a good sign. If he apologised now, she'd give him some slack.

'I did the right thing, bringing you to Havensmere,' he said firmly.

Okay, she wasn't giving him that much slack. 'If that's your idea of an apology it's leaving a little to be desired.'

'I'm not apologising for doing what needed to be done.'

Her stomach muscles clenched even tighter. He wasn't

going to give an inch. The stab of regret made her feel foolish. The man wasn't intriguing. He was a control freak. Clearly they would never get along.

'So I guess that's my cue to leave, then,' she said. But as she stepped past him his hand shot out to stop her.

'Wait.' He held on to her arm. 'You needed your sleep last night—and I didn't want to argue the point when you looked so fragile.' She opened her mouth to speak, but he pressed a finger to her lips. 'Shh, let me finish.' He sighed, letting go of her arm and burying his hands in his back pockets again. 'Despite my concerns about you, I can see I should have asked you first—before I arranged your leave with Parker.'

She obviously wasn't going to get him to be contrite. The rigid line of his jaw made it clear even this much of a concession was costing him. 'Will you promise not to do it again?' she asked.

'Do what, exactly?'

'Make decisions for me without my consent.'

The moment stretched between them before he gave a reluctant nod. 'Okay.' His brow furrowed. 'But I want you to stay the week. Will you?'

She smiled, the questioning look in his eyes making her feel as if she'd just felled Goliath. 'Of course I will. All you had to do was ask me properly.'

He smiled back—and her knees weakened even more, for a very different reason. He touched his thumb to her cheek. 'Good.' He glanced at his watch. 'We're eating on the pool terrace. It's at the back of the house. Ask one of the staff how to get there when you're ready.'

She watched him walk away in silence.

He glanced over his shoulder as he opened the door. 'Don't be long. I'm starving,' he said, then shot her that too-tempting smile again and left.

She frowned at the door as it closed behind him.

Now, why did she get the feeling she hadn't felled Goliath at all, only bruised him a little?

CHAPTER ELEVEN

LOUISA patted the waistline of her linen trousers as she walked down the wide, sweeping staircase to the entrance hall. Was it her imagination or had the waistband got tighter?

Her boot heels gave a sharp crack on the floor of the hall and echoed in the church-like silence. Louisa dropped her head back to look up at the high vaulted ceiling. It finished in a glass dome two storeys above, which flooded the area with natural light. Gold-framed portraits hung on hand-printed silk wallpaper, and carefully positioned Chippendale furniture was polished to an eye-watering gleam. A series of corridors tapered off in different directions, both on the ground level and the one above. Obviously Luke hadn't been kidding when he'd said Havensmere had sixty rooms. He might even have underestimated.

Despite the sparkle of sunlight on the parquet floor, the house was cool. Luke Devereaux's home made her think of Maxim de Winter's Manderlay. Magnificent, but intimidating. Well, at least she had her make-up on at last. The dab of eyeshadow and the dash of lipgloss made her feel bolder and better prepared for what was to come.

She had her armour on now—and she intended to use it.

'Ms DiMarco, it's good to see you up and about.'

Louisa turned at the sound of the soft West Country accent.

A round, ruddy-faced woman walked towards her, wearing a smocked dress, her practical brogues scuffing on the polished floor. 'I'm Mrs Roberts, the head of Mr Devereaux's household staff,' she said, drawing level. She brushed her hand on the apron tied around her waist and offered it to Louisa.

The older woman's grip was firm and hearty, her smile unreserved and welcoming. Luke might be Maxim de Winter, but at least his housekeeper was no Mrs Danvers.

'Hi, I'm Louisa DiMarco—nice to meet you.'

'Nice to meet you too, dear.' The housekeeper's smile broadened. 'Mr Devereaux's waiting for you by the pool. The chef has done a very nice poached salmon for lunch. I'll tell Ellie, our kitchen maid, to serve it now, shall I?'

'Um, that would be great—thanks.' Louisa stumbled over the words, having another Scarlett-down-the-rabbit-hole moment.

The chef? Ellie? How many staff did Devereaux have? He was only one man, for goodness' sake.

The housekeeper reeled off a set of instructions on how to get to the pool terrace in her pleasantly efficient way, and then smiled as her eyes dipped to Louisa's waistline. 'Mr Devereaux has told us your happy news, by the way, so on behalf of the staff here I'd like to congratulate you.'

Louisa gave a tentative smile back, not sure what to say. So Luke had told his staff about the baby. Why did the thought make her feel uneasy?

'We're honoured to have you here, my dear,' the housekeeper continued, still beaming at her as if she'd won the Lottery. 'Anything you need, you let me or one of the other staff know.'

'Thanks—I will.'

Louisa watched the woman leave, feeling more daunted than ever.

She wasn't a complete stranger to the lifestyles of the rich and famous, of course. She worked for one of the most sophisticated women's magazines in the country. She'd been to perfume launches at Claridge's, gone on a PR junket in Manhattan, but she'd never been waited on in her own home.

She'd grown up over her father's north London deli, for goodness' sake, with her whole family crammed into three small bedrooms. She'd never considered herself deprived. But now, as she walked past a series of staid, deathly quiet drawing rooms—all of them larger than her family's entire flat—she wondered how she and her child would fit into Luke Devereaux's world. And whether he could possibly fit into hers.

As she opened the glass-panelled door that led to the gardens she felt like an actress, moments away from her West End debut, who hadn't learned a single one of her lines. Stage fright didn't even begin to cover it. She drew in a deep breath of the flower-scented air and prepared to play the role of her life.

The translucent blue water of the swimming pool sparkled invitingly as she stepped out on the flagstoned terrace. She spotted Luke on the other side of the pool, seated at an elaborate wrought-iron table shaded under a leafy chestnut tree. A young woman in a black maid's uniform was laying out a selection of plates and platters as he read his newspaper.

The fine china, the lacy linen tablecloth and her devastatingly handsome host were all so perfect her pulse spiked again. If it hadn't been for Luke's faded jeans the scene would have looked like something out of a Renoir painting.

Le Déjeuner sur l'Herbe deluxe, Louisa thought wryly.

She watched as Luke gave the girl a curt nod. The maid nodded back and left. No wonder he had that take-charge attitude. He'd obviously been born and bred to give orders and to have them obeyed instantly. She smoothed her hair down. Well, he wasn't going to order her around—not any more.

Her boot heels clattered on the stone tiles and he glanced over his shoulder. She could have sworn she felt all those centuries of power in his gaze as it raked over her. He folded his paper and stood up as she approached—the epitome of aristocratic gallantry. The impeccable manners didn't fool her, though. She knew how quickly the veneer of civilisation disappeared whenever he was challenged— or aroused.

He gestured to the poached salmon displayed on a bed of exotic salad leaves. 'I hope you're hungry. Leonard has prepared enough for an army,' he said, those penetrating silver eyes locking on her face.

Her breathing got a little choppy, and her heart skipped a beat. Stop it, woman. He's just a man and you're his equal, not his subordinate, whatever he might think.

'It looks delicious,' she said, grateful the rumble in her stomach was disguised by the rustle of leaves.

She sat stiffly in her chair and observed him as he seated himself and began serving their meal. No wonder she'd found him irresistible that night, when she'd thought he was a regular guy. Being in this mansion, though, would remind her every day that he was anything but. He was an aristocrat, a lord of the realm, a man far too used to being the master of all he surveyed.

She picked up a monogrammed napkin and spread it over her lap.

She was going to have quite a job on her hands teaching Luke Devereaux he was not the master of her. With that in mind, she ought to keep her hormones under better control than she had this morning. Jumping into bed with Luke whenever he clicked his fingers probably wasn't the best way to give him a lesson in humility or convince him she wasn't his latest toy.

Luke watched as his guest forked up some salmon and slid the pale pink flesh into her mouth. Oil slicked her bottom lip and her tongue darted out to lick it off. He accepted the familiar punch of lust with a half-smile.

Louisa DiMarco was easily the most troublesome woman he'd ever met, but there was no denying she fascinated him. He wasn't used to women standing up to him the way she had, and he couldn't recall the last time one had said no to him—especially when it was obvious she wanted to say yes. That she was pregnant with his child raised the stakes—but as far as he could see it didn't alter them. Once this tantalising battle of wills was over he intended to have his child properly provided for and Louisa DiMarco right where he wanted her.

He lifted the icy jug of homemade lemonade and poured them both a glass. He brought the glass to his lips and let the cold, tangy liquid slide down his throat as he contemplated his opponent. He'd expected she'd object to the decision he'd made about their future this morning. But he'd worked out a strategy and this time he was sticking to it. She'd got him so stirred up earlier he'd lost control of the situation for a moment. He wasn't going to make that mistake again.

He was the hunter here, not her—and he wasn't about to get captured by the game.

CHAPTER TWELVE

LOUISA dug into her meal with gusto. She really had been famished, and the delicious fare helped to bolster her spirits. It couldn't do a great deal for the little jumps in her stomach, though.

Her host didn't seem to mind the silence, making no attempt to fill the gap with pointless small talk. But several times she looked up from her plate to find him watching her—and the little jumps got a whole lot bigger.

His watchfulness reminded her of their first night together. He hadn't talked much then either—apart from the odd wry quip. Probably one of the reasons she knew so little about him now. Most of the time he'd looked and listened, with a concentration that had been a major turn on at the time.

Afterwards she'd assumed his apparent fascination with her had all been an act, but now she knew better. It was all part of that single-mindedness that was an integral part of his personality. He'd wanted her that night so he'd gone after her—seducing her with a ruthless efficiency that had left her powerless to resist him. And he'd come pretty close to doing the same thing this morning.

As she finished her meal, she began to wonder what his

next move was going to be. Did he have a plan of action for their baby all figured out?

She ignored the ripple of panic. Remember you're setting the agenda now. Not him.

'Louisa, I've been thinking about our situation—with the baby.'

Her fork clattered onto her plate. Good grief, had he just read her mind?

'Oh, really?' she said, as casually as she could manage. Why was he looking at her so intently? She felt a barrage of butterflies flutter to life in her stomach. Obviously the pleasantries were over with.

'I have an obvious solution that should satisfy us both,' he said easily.

I can just imagine. She picked up her glass to buy time. 'That sounds intriguing.'

'We should get married.'

The sip of lemonade Louisa had just swallowed hit her tonsils as shock reverberated through her. She tried to grab a breath as a coughing fit raked her body. He passed her his napkin, leaning over to pat her back, cooler than any cucumber.

Eventually the hacking coughs stopped. His warm palm stayed heavy on her spine.

'Everything all right?' he asked calmly—too calmly for a man who ought to be certified.

She nodded, not quite able to speak.

He leaned back in his chair and crossed his legs, resting one ankle on his knee. He studied her. 'It's the obvious solution. It's important to me to give the baby my name, and I intend to support you both.' His lips lifted in a sensual smile. 'I don't think it would be a hardship for either of us to spend time together in the months ahead—our schedules permitting.'

'Have you completely lost your marbles?' she croaked.

He sighed. 'Somehow I guessed you wouldn't do this the easy way.'

She didn't like the condescending tone, but decided to ignore it. Surely he couldn't have thought this through? 'Luke, we hardly know each other. The idea of us getting married is preposterous.'

'So we get to know each other once we're married.'

'No,' she said, the butterflies ready to fly right out of her ears. He was actually serious about this.

His eyebrow winged up. 'What do you mean, no?'

'No, I'm not marrying you.'

Annoyance flashed in his eyes.

She had the errant thought that this wasn't how it was supposed to be. As a girl she'd fantasised often about how the man of her dreams was going to sweep her off her feet when he asked her to marry him—and Luke Devereaux's perfunctory proposal didn't even come close.

There was supposed to be a diamond ring, flowers, flickering candlelight and romance. Louisa dismissed the sharp stab of disappointment as self-pity. She had more important things to deal with right now than shattered dreams.

'You're having my child,' he said, as if he were dictating a business memo. 'We know each other well enough.'

'Luke, we've spent less than a full day in each other's company—and we've spent most of the time arguing,' she finished with an exasperated huff.

He laughed. 'Not all of the time, though.' His hand covered hers on the table, making her jump. 'You wouldn't be pregnant now if we had.'

She felt the sizzle of awareness as his thumb brushed the back of her hand. She grabbed her hand away, buried it in her lap.

'Sexual attraction isn't enough for a marriage.' She fisted her hands. So much for setting the agenda. He'd just torpedoed her modest little scheme—to see how they got along in the coming days—right out of the water.

'It's a start,' he said, the beguiling smile making her heart stutter. 'One we can build on.'

She cocked her head to one side, and a little spurt of hope wheedled its way past the panic. Was this his heavy-handed way of saying he wanted to give their relationship a chance?

'We don't have to get married to get to know each other,' she said.

'Yes, we do,' he said. 'There's a child involved, remember?'

She frowned. Had she time-travelled back to the Victorian era? 'In case you haven't noticed, we're living in the twenty-first century, not the nineteenth. Children are born out of wedlock all the time.'

He straightened, and the tempting smile disappeared. 'Not my children.'

She'd hit a nerve—and the urge to probe was irresistible. Maybe she'd finally get an answer to the question that had been bugging her since he'd stormed into her office. 'Why not your children? Why are you so determined to give this baby your name?'

Was it possible that he already loved it? Wanted it as much as she did?

'Because it's mine,' he said coldly.

The hope fizzled out. It wasn't the answer she'd been looking for. 'The baby's a person. It doesn't belong to anyone.'

'I know that,' he said, but there was still no warmth in his voice. 'I want it to have my name. To achieve that we have to get married.'

'No, we don't,' she said, silently amazed at how stubborn he was being. 'You could be named on the birth certificate as the father. There's no need to—'

'That would still make it a bastard,' he interrupted. 'It's not an option. We have to get married.'

She heard the tiny crack in his voice, noticed the hard line of his jaw and realised this was more than stubbornness. 'Luke, marriage is a lifelong commitment—or it should be. I'm not prepared to have a marriage of convenience with someone I hardly know to pander to some out-of-date sense of propriety.'

He gave a harsh laugh. 'Louisa, you're not what anyone would call *convenient*.'

The casual barb stung. 'Well, neither are you. Which is all the more reason not to…'

'Okay, okay.' He lifted his hand to silence her. 'We'd better not argue about this. It'll only turn us on.'

She gasped. How could he be so crass? She opened her mouth to object, but he propped his elbow on the table and skimmed his hand down her hair. The tenderness of the gesture and the fierce approval in his gaze shocked her so much she lost her train of thought.

'We've got a week,' he said gently, his hand cupping her cheek. 'I say we use the time to get to know each other.' His thumb pressed her bottom lip. 'In every way possible.'

He traced his thumb down the side of her neck. Her breath gushed out, the pulse of arousal detonating at her core. She grasped his hand, dragged it away from her face.

She wanted to take what he offered at face value, but

she'd been burnt once before by her overwhelming attraction to this man and she knew she couldn't. Where sex was involved he had a power over her she wasn't sure she could control—and she wasn't about to be seduced into marriage.

'I'm not going to pretend I don't want to sleep with you,' she murmured. He'd know she was lying. 'But I need time. I'm not going to be rushed. We're virtual strangers, Luke—and that scares me.'

His brow wrinkled. 'How much time? We've only got a week.'

'I'm not sure,' she said. 'But I want a truce tonight. I'm still shattered from yesterday.'

It wasn't strictly speaking the truth. She was a little tired, but what was bothering her a lot more was the sudden swirl of conflicting emotions at his marriage proposal. Her mind had rejected it out of hand, but in some small corner of her heart she could feel a tiny little flicker of expectancy, of excitement, which could easily flare out of control if she wasn't careful.

'What kind of truce?' He eyed her suspiciously.

'No more talking about sex,' she replied quickly. 'And no touching.'

His eyebrows shot up and then he laughed. 'Don't be ridiculous,' he said. 'We're not schoolchildren.'

She stood, brushed off her trousers to disguise the trembling in her hands. 'Fine, if that's the way you feel then I'll see you for breakfast tomorrow morning.'

He got up too and snagged her wrist. 'What are you planning to do?' he teased. 'Lock yourself in your room?'

She thrust her chin out. 'If I have to.' She hoped she sounded as if she meant it. The feel of his thumb rubbing the inside of her wrist wasn't doing much for her resolve.

'I need some alone time this afternoon. But I'll come down for dinner if you promise not to pressure me. I'm not sleeping with you tonight. I'm not ready.'

He scanned her face, still stroking. Could he feel the betraying rabbit punches of her pulse? She hoped not.

'Fine,' he said at last. 'If you're sure that's what you want.' He lifted a sceptical eyebrow.

'I'm absolutely positive that's what I want,' she lied.

She tried to step past him, but his fingers remained clamped on her wrist. 'Not so fast,' he said. 'I want a promise in return.'

'What is it?' she said, the blasted rabbit now pummelling her wrist as if it was training for the world heavyweight boxing championships.

'I won't touch as long as you don't.' There was that seductive smile again, and the promise of something particularly carnal in his eyes.

Her knees went to jelly.

She nodded, knowing she couldn't trust her voice.

Who had won that round? she wondered as she walked away on unsteady legs.

Given her senses were already in full revolt at the prospect of the evening's 'no-touch' ordeal, she had the distinct impression it wasn't her. Somehow the wily, intractable and devilishly sexy Lord Berwick had got the better of her again.

What she needed now was sensible, partisan advice from someone who knew what they were talking about. Her best friend Mel Rourke Devlin had two children and five years of marital bliss with a gorgeous husband who had once virtually kidnapped her too. If Mel didn't know what Louisa should do now, no one would.

Time to use her 'phone a friend' option.

* * *

Luke watched Louisa cross the flagstones and glimpsed the edge of purple underwear peeping over the waistband of her hip-hugging trousers. He imagined running his thumb into the sensitive hollow of her spine and under the lace. He forced his eyes away, sat back down at the table and picked up his paper, the kick of arousal making a slow smile spread across his face.

The proposal had gone better than he'd expected.

His solicitor was the one who'd suggested marriage during their phone call that morning. Luke had balked at the idea at first himself, but had quickly accepted the fact that marriage was the only answer.

Despite Louisa's refusal, he knew he'd get his ring on her finger in the end. Failure wasn't an option—not after what he'd gone through as a child. But he could see now the process of getting Louisa to co-operate wasn't going to be as much of a chore as he'd first thought.

He scanned the shares columns, but the numbers blurred as he contemplated Louisa's changing expressions during their lunch—shocked, defiant, confused, and finally desperately turned on.

She could have the so-called truce she wanted tonight, he conceded magnanimously. He was a man of his word, and he never pressured women into bed—however much he might want to.

But that didn't mean he couldn't make tonight as agonising for her as it was going to be for him.

CHAPTER THIRTEEN

'PREPARE yourself for a shock, Mel.' Louisa's hands shook as she gripped her mobile phone. 'I'm pregnant, and Luke Devereaux is the father.'

Louisa heard her friend's gasp, and then the crackle of static as she fumbled the phone.

'Oh, my God!' Mel shouted down the line. 'I *knew* something happened that night. I knew it. But you were so adamant, and I was—' She stopped in mid-stream. 'Wait a minute. That dinner party was three months ago. Why didn't you tell me? I asked you last week. When you said you'd been feeling sick and your bra didn't fit I asked you if you could be pregnant and you said no way.'

'Because I didn't know.'

'Don't be ridiculous. How could you not know you were—?'

'It's a long, boring story,' Louisa interrupted. And one she wasn't about to go into now.

'Okay,' Mel replied. 'So when's the baby due?'

The simple, sincere question had tears pooling in Louisa's eyes. Emotion hit her like a tidal wave as she remembered exactly why she loved Mel—and how much she needed her now. She sniffed, tried to think. 'It's due the second week in February.'

'Lou, are you crying?'

'It's these flipping hormones,' Louisa said, swiping at her eyes. 'Mel, the thing is, the baby's not the only shock.'

'What do you mean?'

'I'm at Luke's country house at the moment,' Louisa said, deciding she ought to lead up to shock number two gradually. Mel was seven months pregnant, after all.

'What's it like?' Mel asked eagerly. 'I've heard it's incredible.'

'It's unbelievable. Like Buckingham Palace.' She paused to look round the beautifully appointed bedroom suite again. 'But more classy.'

'That's fantastic.' Mel gave an excited giggle. 'So, you guys are an item, then?'

'It's a bit more complicated than that.' She swallowed heavily, gathering her courage. 'He's asked me to marry him. Or rather he's *told* me to marry him.'

There was complete silence on the other end of the line. Louisa could almost hear Mel's brain clicking into overdrive.

'Good grief,' her friend said at last, sounding stunned. 'Will that make you Lady Berwick, then?'

'Don't be daft. I'm not *actually* going to marry him. That would be insane.'

'Why on earth not?' Mel said bluntly. 'He's the father of your baby, he's gorgeous, and I could have sworn I read somewhere that he's one of the most eligible bachelors in Britain. Now, I wonder where I read that?'

Louisa couldn't believe the levity in Mel's voice. 'Mel, this is not funny. He kidnapped me—and now he's planning to seduce me into marrying him. I feel like I've been sucked into a penny-dreadful novel. What am I supposed to do?'

'Oh, come off it, Lou,' Mel scoffed, obviously still unaware of the gravity of the situation. 'There's nothing dreadful about Luke Devereaux. He's a total studmuffin. Even Ella is besotted with him, and you know how picky she is.'

'Ella's five!' Louisa said, shocked that Mel would talk about her daughter that way.

'True,' Mel said, still sounding amused. 'And I don't think she's quite ready to dump Ken for him yet, but she did try to sit on his lap last time he was here.' Mel's voice sobered. 'The point is she likes him—and she's an excellent judge of character. And you must like him too, or you wouldn't have got pregnant. So why are you so horrified at the prospect of marrying him?'

Louisa sighed. How did she even begin to describe how she felt about Luke Devereaux?

'I'm not horrified. I'm terrified. What if I fall in love with him?' The words popped out of her mouth before she'd even known they were there.

'Oh, Lou.' The gentle exclamation held a wealth of sympathy and understanding. 'I know falling in love can be terrifying. But it's also the most wonderful thing in the world.'

'Not if he doesn't love you back,' she blurted out, and then felt pathetic. 'And not if you're completely incompatible.' Which was the real problem. 'We've only spent a day or so together, and we've already got enough issues to start an election campaign.'

'What issues?' Mel said, in her usual cut-to-the-chase fashion.

At last they were getting somewhere. 'Well, for starters getting personal information out of him is harder than breaking into Fort Knox.' Louisa paced over to the window. 'And he's a complete control freak—he expects to have everything his own way and doesn't know the meaning of the word *compromise*.' She took a breath, gathering speed.

'Plus, whenever I make a perfectly valid objection to his behaviour he deliberately distracts me—with sex.'

'The rotter,' Mel said, that suspicious lift in her voice again.

'Don't you dare laugh.'

'I know, I know. It's not funny. But, Lou, just tell me one thing. Is it good sex?'

'It's fantastic sex, but that's not the point.'

'He passed the Meg Ryan Test, didn't he?'

Why on earth had she told Mel about the Meg Ryan Test? No wonder no one took her seriously. She was an idiot. 'So what if he did? That's not enough to make us a good match.'

'Yes, but it's a very good start.'

Mel's words echoed Luke's so closely Louisa wanted to scream. Before she could start she heard a crash on the line, and then Mel shouted, 'Ella Valentine Devlin—stop that this instant!'

After two minutes of muffled wailing, Mel came back on the line. 'Lou, I'm really sorry, but I can't talk long. Ella's given Cal a make-over with her felt-tip pens and woken him from his nap.'

Louisa could hear the toddler's babbling and guessed he was on Mel's hip. 'Don't worry, I'm fine. I'll figure it out,' she said, feeling more overwhelmed than ever.

'Don't panic, Lou. This is my advice, for what it's worth.' Another toddler babble, and then Mel's calming *shhh*. 'I understand why the idea of marriage has freaked you out. It's a lot to handle along with a new baby, and it does seem a little extreme if you hardly know each other.'

'My point exactly.' Finally her friend was getting the picture.

'I'm assuming you told him no?' Mel said carefully.

'I tried to. He doesn't exactly take no for an answer, though.'

'So what are your plans?'

'I said I'd stay the week.'

'You are sleeping together, then?'

'Not quite.' But they soon would be.

'Why not, if the sex is fantastic?'

Why not indeed? 'I don't know. I panicked. He's so overpowering. I didn't want to get swept away, so I told him he couldn't touch me tonight.' She winced. Luke was right, her request sounded juvenile.

But Mel just giggled. 'That's brilliant.'

'It is?'

'From what you've said, and the little I know about him myself, Luke Devereaux's a guy who needs to be kicked right out of his comfort zone before he'll let his guard down. If he distracts you with sex, why not distract him right back?'

A little flicker of excitement leapt up to Louisa's breastbone and started doing the hula. 'Mel, are you mad? It would never work.' But then she stopped to consider Mel's idea. The truth was, she'd tried outrage and indignation and even common sense and it had been a disaster—not to mention extremely unsatisfying. 'How do you suggest I pull that off without bursting into flames?'

'Phooey,' Mel said. 'You know how. You're the best flirt in the Western World when you put your mind to it. Trust me, the guy's toast.'

After her conversation with Mel, Louisa resolved to stay busy during the afternoon. She didn't want to go into meltdown before she saw Luke again. If she was even going to consider attempting what Mel had suggested she had to stay calm and focussed—or as calm and focussed as was humanly possible, given that she was practically on fire.

She spoke to Mrs Roberts and arranged to have one of Luke's employees pop into her flat and get some clothes couriered down for the rest of her stay. She lay on the bed and tried to have a mid-afternoon nap, but after seventeen solid hours the night before and the anticipation making all her pulse points throb she couldn't close her eyes without seeing that tempting, challenging look in Luke's eyes at lunchtime. So she gave up trying.

She slipped down the corridor while the coast was clear and found the library Mrs Roberts had mentioned—which looked like something out of *My Fair Lady*—and used one of the computers there to research the first few months of pregnancy on the internet.

Discovering she was unlikely to suffer from more morning sickness at this late date was the good news. Finding out about heartburn, stretch marks, oedema, pre-eclampsia and the host of other ailments she might have to negotiate in the months to come was the bad. She felt she'd been holding up well at the enormity of it all when she stumbled across a picture of a foetus at six months. Tears flooded her eyes. She switched the terminal off and sniffed them back. All these things were inevitable, and she was sure she'd do just fine. She was fit, supremely healthy, and took good care of herself—now she knew she was looking after two people instead of one she would be extra careful.

Getting up from the desk, she glanced through the long mullioned windows. It was approaching six o'clock and the light had taken on an early-evening glow, softening the iridescent green of the summer landscape to a deep emerald. The house was surrounded by landscaped gardens, but instead of the ordered selection of cultured blooms one might expect in a stately home, the flowers of Havensmere spilled out of their beds in cosy, comforting disarray. Lupins and buddleia vyed for attention with roses and dahlias, like ladies at a garden party flirting with their beaus. The image made Louisa smile. The place really was idyllic, for all its grandeur.

She wondered if Luke had selected any of the flowers, then dismissed the idea. Not only did he seem far too macho to know anything about flowers, she couldn't imagine him spending his time doing anything as humble as gardening. It didn't fit with that slick, sophisticated, captain of industry image he had going for him.

She flattened her hand against the pane, felt the heat of the day through the glass, and the buzz of anticipation pulsed even hotter under her skin. She could see the edge of the pool from this angle. The turquoise water lapped against the pale blue mosaic tiles and she imagined diving in to the cool, inviting depths. Mrs Roberts had told her they had a selection of new swimming costumes in the pool house for the use of the guests if she wanted to take a dip. The idea suddenly seemed unbearably appealing.

But did she dare take a swim? What would happen if Luke spotted her practically naked and dripping wet?

A giddy laugh popped out of her mouth, the throaty chuckle echoing round the cavernous room as the hula-dancers sashayed right up her throat. It would be dangerous, reckless—tantamount to tempting the devil. She'd be playing with fire, but somehow the danger only tantalised her more.

Mel was right. Luke Devereaux needed to be kicked out of his comfort zone. Way out. He'd given his word that he wouldn't touch her tonight, probably expecting her to be

some meek little wallflower who'd be available for pluck-
ing when he felt like it.

But why shouldn't she take the initiative for once? So
long as she kept her hands to herself he'd be at a distinct
disadvantage because of his promise earlier—which was
just where she wanted him.

So far he'd called all the shots in their little battle of the
sexes. But she had some powerful ammunition too and it
was way past time she started shooting back.

She peered down the corridor as she left the library,
making absolutely sure Luke wasn't lurking anywhere.
She wanted maximum impact for her little show.

She planned to have the benefit of surprise when she
fired her opening volley.

He wouldn't know what had hit him.

'No, hold off on dumping the Westling shares. The price
is going to peak on Monday or Tuesday. Don't sell before
they touch twenty.' Luke gave a few absent grunts of assent
and struggled to concentrate as his broker in New York
reeled through a series of figures. He'd been on the phone
for over two hours to his fund managers around the globe,
getting weekly reports on his various stock options. It was
a task he usually revelled in.

He had a mathematician's love of numbers, and an
almost clairvoyant ability to predict what shares would go
up and which would go down, and the steeliest nerve in
the business. He adored the cut and thrust of the financial
markets, the rush of adrenalin that came from knowing he
could wipe out a life's work or make billions in a single
heartbeat. And his passion for the fray had made him rich.
But this afternoon the gambler's zeal that usually made
him so eager to discuss his investments had all but deserted

him. For the first time ever making money felt like a chore. And he knew exactly whose fault that was. Miss Louisa DiMarco. The contrary little minx had grabbed all his attention in the last few weeks—hell, the last few months— and since bringing her to Havensmere her effect on him had only got worse.

He strolled across the study as his broker's voice droned on down the line from Manhattan. The list of figures was failing to engage him in the least.

He glanced absently out the window, spotted the woman levering herself out of the pool and almost dropped the phone.

'Hell!' he breathed, his fingers tightening on the handset as all the blood drained out of his head and shot straight to his groin.

Luke stared as the bane of his existence sauntered across the flagstone patio. Naturally poised, her leggy gait was as fluid and confident as any catwalk model—except this woman had curves where she was supposed to have curves. Luke swallowed convulsively, the voice of his broker receding to a distant hum.

Water ran in rivulets down Louisa's dusky skin and glittered in the sunlight. The two minuscule scraps of scarlet material she wore clung to lush breasts and left absolutely nothing to his imagination. She reached one of the loungers and picked up a towel. Dropping her head back, she swayed it from side to side, sprinkling the parched tiles. He watched, riveted to the spot, as she grasped the long dark-blonde hair falling in wet tangles down her back, leaned to one side and squeezed it like a hunk of rope. The movement made her breasts strain against the tiny bow that fastened her bikini top.

Luke eased out a breath, the vicious ache in his groin throbbing harder as he pictured himself untying the bow and letting those ripe breasts sway into his waiting palms.

He swung away from the window, forced himself to walk back to his desk and sit down. He adjusted his jeans in a pointless attempt to accommodate the erection pressed against the fly.

The broker was still talking to him. 'Look, sorry…' he interrupted, then hesitated. He'd worked with this guy for five years and he couldn't remember his name. 'Patrick,' he said at last, hoping the mild guess was correct. 'We'll have to pick this up tomorrow. Something has come up.'

He winced. Something had come up all right, and it didn't feel as if it was going to be going down again any time soon. He finished the call, drummed his fingers on the desk, thought about giving Louisa her privacy for about five seconds, and then shot straight back over to the window.

She was drying herself in slow, careful strokes. First those mile-long legs—bringing the towel up the inside of her thigh and making the breath catch in his throat. Then she glided it down her arms and finally brought it to rest under her breasts. She held the heavy orbs in her palms for a few seconds—that felt like a lifetime—and his heartbeat slowed to a dull throb as her thumbnail scraped across the scarlet Lycra. Even one storey up he could have sworn he saw the nipple peak against the clingy fabric.

He scrubbed open palms down his face. This was humiliating. He felt like a twelve year old boy hiding under the covers to ogle his first nude centrefold magazine, but he couldn't take his eyes off her and end the torment. She'd throw a fit if she knew he was spying on her. But just as the thought registered she lifted her head, her hands still plumping up those delicious breasts, and stared straight at him.

The saucy smile that spread over her face held all the self-satisfied allure of Salome dancing the *Seven Veils*.

'Why, you…' he rasped, his tongue numb from the shock.

She winked at him, flipped the towel over her shoulder and blew him a cheeky kiss before turning round and sashaying towards the terrace doors. His gaze glued itself to her perfectly rounded bottom, spotlighted in scarlet as it jiggled out of view.

Despite the pulsating ache in his crotch, and the thought of the ice-cold shower he was going to have to endure before dinnertime, he choked out a laugh.

He had to hand it to her. The crafty little siren had got him good.

Which meant he would be honour-bound to get her right back tonight.

Even if it killed him.

CHAPTER FOURTEEN

'YOU'RE going to cook?' Louisa stared at Luke, unable to hide her astonishment. 'But I thought…' That they would be dining in the ballroom-sized dining salon she had spotted that afternoon—with his staff in attendance.

One dark brow lifted and his lips twitched. 'It's the staff's night off,' he said, doing his mind-reading thing again. 'We've got the place to ourselves.' He nodded down the corridor behind her as his silver eyes raked over the little black dress she wore. 'We'll eat in the conservatory. It's more intimate.'

Oops, she thought, every one of her nerve-endings tingling alarmingly. When she'd planned her display by the pool she hadn't realised she was going to be alone in the dragon's den tonight.

He had yet to mention her stunt, which she'd taken as a great sign. Power had surged through her when their eyes had locked earlier. The thought that he had been forced to change his strategy had made the wild rush even more intoxicating. But now she could see she'd underestimated him. He didn't seem fazed in the least.

He inclined his head in a shallow bow and held his arm out. 'Shall we?' he said, waiting for her to precede him.

As soon as she'd passed him, though, the hot weight of his palm settled on her lower back. Her pulse scrambled. Should she mention their no-touching agreement? Or would it be a sign of weakness so early in the game?

He had to let her go to push open the wide double doors at the end of the hallway. She bit her lip to hold back the sigh of relief.

As she stepped into the room she was momentarily distracted by the beauty of the airy space. A multi-faceted conservatory filled the open-plan kitchen with natural light given a redolent glow by the approaching twilight. She could see the gardens beyond, laid out in a dizzying collection of psychedelic summer colours. A raft of glass-fronted cabinets and grey slate work surfaces lined the walls and made the room look both inviting and glaringly modern.

Louisa gaped. She'd been expecting something older and less sophisticated, probably because she'd assumed the kitchen was a part of the house he would never see or use. 'This is gorgeous,' she said.

'I'm glad you approve,' he said, the husky rumble whispering across her earlobe. She spun round and nearly smacked into his chest. He steadied her, but his large palm stayed on her hip, holding her in place.

She stepped back, dislodging it. 'You're not supposed to touch me, or have you forgotten your promise already?' Annoyingly, the accusation came out on a breathy murmur.

His lips twitched again. 'After the show you put on for me this afternoon, you're lucky I don't spank you.'

He was teasing her, she knew that, but the heady thrill at the threat still shocked her. She hated to be under someone else's control, had always rebelled against it. But now she had to admit his dominant nature excited her as much as it annoyed her.

'Spank me if you want,' she said defiantly. 'But I expect to be fed first. I'm starving.'

His eyes darkened like a summer storm and she wondered if she'd gone too far. But then he gave an astonished chuckle. 'Fine—food first.' He drew her to him, gave her rump a firm pat. 'Spanking later,' he finished, and walked past her into the kitchen.

As his steps echoed on the slate flooring she could feel the sizzle on her buttocks and realised it was going to be a struggle to eat a single bite.

'Now, let's see what we've got to play with.'

She turned at the suggestive statement to see him bending over to check out the contents of the industrial-sized refrigerator. Worn denim stretched lovingly across a very nice male behind. She gave a muffled groan. She must not fantasise about playing with that—not just yet anyway. Or she'd be the one who was toast, not him.

He stood up, holding a selection of salad vegetables and a shrink-wrapped package. 'How about steak and salad?'

'Sounds delicious,' she said, barely able to stop from licking her lips at the sight of all that rampant maleness confined in the cosy domestic setting.

'Have you had any cravings yet?' he asked as he dropped the food on the kitchen counter.

Quite a few actually, she thought, noticing the way his T-shirt stretched across his chest as he pulled a drawer open. 'Only for the usual,' she said.

He stopped rummaging. 'Such as?'

'Chocolate muffins, chocolate ice cream and—well, just plain chocolate,' she babbled. 'I'm going to have to be careful I don't end up weighing twenty stone before this is over.'

He tilted his head, swept his eyes down her frame,

lingered for a moment on her bosom. 'Don't worry,' he said, lifting his gaze to her face, his eyes shining devilishly. 'I've got the perfect way to keep you in shape.'

Heat pooled low in her abdomen—and just like that the sexual tension rocketed right back up to fever pitch. This was going to be the longest night of her life—and she had only herself to blame.

He ripped the wrapping off the steak, placed the meat on the chopping board, ground some salt and pepper over it and then began to rub the seasoning in.

Her cheeks warmed. 'Why don't I set the table?' she said. *So I can stop thinking about those long, strong fingers massaging naked flesh.*

He glanced up, the expression on his face telling her he knew exactly what she was thinking. 'Is it too hot for you in here?' he asked, making the casual enquiry sound like a dare.

'Not at all,' she said, determined not to fold. 'I know— why don't I chop the cucumber?'

Two can play at that game, buster.

She picked up the long, decidedly phallic vegetable and stroked the length of it. 'Mmm, I adore cucumber,' she said in a husky whisper. 'Fresh, firm and so tasty.' She fluttered her eyelashes and did her best porn-star pout.

He groaned. 'Put the damn cucumber down and go and lay the table in the conservatory,' he demanded, his tone strained. 'The cutlery's in the drawer by the fridge,' he said, nodding across the kitchen.

She couldn't resist a smug little smile as she walked into the glass atrium and heard the sharp raps of his knife on the chopping board as he decimated the cucumber.

Touché.

The profusion of flowers and climbing vines winding

around the trellis cocooned an iron gate-legged table and chairs and made the conservatory look like a fairytale bower.

She breathed in the heady perfume and sighed. 'You should give your gardener a medal,' she said absently as she put the silverware down. 'The choice of flowers and plants on this estate is amazing.'

The chopping stopped. 'I designed the gardens,' he said.

She spun round. 'Are you serious?'

He didn't say anything, didn't even spare her a glance as he walked over to the stove, laid the steak on the hot griddle. 'I like gardening,' he said eventually, above the sizzle of frying meat, but she could still hear the twinge of embarrassment in his tone.

What a surprise. Maybe Mr Macho had hidden depths after all.

She finished setting the table and sat down to watch him cook. He flipped the steaks over and sprinkled herbs on them, then tossed the salad and added dressing—all with the skill and efficiency of a professional chef.

Was there nothing this man didn't excel at? And when had that relaxed confidence become sexy instead of intimidating?

Louisa's mouth began to water, and it wasn't from the captivating aroma of sautéed meat.

'That was delicious,' Louisa said, pushing her plate away. Despite the hum of arousal in her stomach, she'd made indecently short work of the steak and freshly dressed salad Luke had prepared.

'Glad to be of service.' Luke studied her as he took a sip of his mineral water—and she knew the brief respite was over. 'If you're still hungry I can probably dig up some chocolate ice cream,' he added.

'Don't tempt me,' she said, her throat dry.

He smiled, that slow, sensuous smile that did funny things to her insides—and she knew chocolate ice cream was the least of the temptations on offer. His eyes deepened, the twinkle of amusement gone, obliterated by something much more dangerous. 'Ready for your spanking yet?'

She put his empty plate on top of her own and stood. Damn, her knees were wobbling again. 'I'll clean up first, and then we can discuss it,' she said flippantly, pleased with herself when the plates barely rattled.

But he got up and lifted the crockery out of her hands. 'Leave it,' he said. 'You're going to need your strength, sweetheart.'

Oh, good grief, what was wrong with her? Her thighs had gone liquid now too.

He pulled her easily into his arms and she inhaled his scent—soap and man and something else equally delicious. Her nostrils flared as she felt the jolt of awareness right down to her toes.

She wedged her hands between them, but couldn't muster the will to push him away.

His hands strayed down to her behind and he squeezed. 'I hate to punish you, you know,' he said, his voice rough as his lips nuzzled the hollow below her ear and his fingers stroked. 'But sometimes a man's gotta do what a man's gotta do.'

She edged back. 'I'm starting to worry about this obsession you have with corporal punishment, Devereaux,' she teased, loving the way the blue-grey of his eyes had darkened to a rich cobalt. 'I hope you realise how kinky it is, even for someone born into the British aristocracy.'

He hauled her against him, giving a low chuckle. 'I wasn't born into the British aristocracy,' he murmured, his lips doing incredible things to her earlobe. 'I was born a Vegas street rat. My mother worked the floorshow at Ceasar's Palace.'

The vicious arousal dimmed as her mind locked onto the startling information. She wriggled back, stared at him. 'Your mother was a showgirl in Vegas? You're kidding?'

He looked at her blankly for a moment, cursed quietly, and dropped his hands as if he'd been burned.

Hell—had he just said that out loud?

Luke raked his fingers through his hair, registering Louisa's inquisitive look and the sharp intelligence in her gaze. He'd been about to devour those full lips of hers in a few quick, greedy bites. And then he'd told her about his mother! Obviously the sexual frustration of the last few days had finally melted his brain cells.

'Go out on the terrace. I'll make us some coffee,' he said tightly, feeling as if he'd stuck his head in a noose. He never talked about his background. Not to anyone.

'Don't change the subject,' she said, prodding her finger into his chest. 'You can't drop a bombshell like that into a conversation and then expect it not to detonate.'

'That wasn't a conversation, it was foreplay—so anything I said doesn't count. Forget it,' he said, trying to keep the desperation out of his voice. 'I'm not discussing this. It'll ruin the mood.' He grasped her wrist and pulled her against him. 'If you don't want coffee that's fine. We'll just pick up where we left off.'

But as he lowered his head to kiss her, she pressed her fingers to his lips.

'If your mother was a Vegas showgirl how did you end up becoming Berwick's heir?' she asked, her eyes bright with curiosity.

'Oh, for…' He swore again and stepped back. He couldn't believe this. They'd been on the brink of tearing each other's clothes off and now she wanted to talk. She had to be the most infuriating woman ever. 'I don't want to talk about this, and I especially don't want to talk about it now. It's boring as hell, and we've got better things to do.'

Why was he having to point out the obvious? She'd been as eager as he had a moment ago.

'There's no need to shout, Luke,' she said. 'And you know I'm not sleeping with you tonight. So all this kissing is probably a bad idea anyway. It'll only frustrate us both.'

He blinked, completely flabbergasted. 'You're not serious? Why the hell won't you sleep with me tonight? And don't tell me you don't want to.'

Her cheeks pinkened but she looked him dead in the eye. 'I already told you this afternoon. I want to know more about you before I take that leap again.'

She *was* serious. She'd turned him on to the point of madness and now she wasn't going to follow through. 'You know what you are, Louisa?' He snarled the words, glaring at her. 'You're a bloody tease.'

If he was expecting remorse, he didn't get it.

She didn't even flinch at the insult. 'That is so typical of a man.' She splayed her hand on her hip and glared right back at him. 'It must be so convenient having that old double standard to fall back on every time you don't get what you want.'

'What are you talking about now?' His head was about to explode.

'You're allowed to use sex as a weapon because you're a guy, but if I do it I'm a tease.'

'I never used sex as a weapon.'

'Yes, you did,' she said, stabbing him in the chest again to make her point. 'What were all those smouldering looks about, then? The touching? The kissing? The innuendo?'

He grabbed her finger. Leaned down until their faces were nose to nose. 'Yeah, but the difference is I had every intention of following through,' he murmured, his voice low with menace. He knew he was bullying her, but he couldn't seem to stop himself. He wanted her and she wanted him. Why should they wait any longer?

She tugged her hand out of his. 'I didn't say I wasn't going to follow through. I know where all this is leading. I'm not an idiot.' She was visibly shaking now, those chocolate-brown eyes vivid with passion and temper. He hadn't cowed her at all, he realised. The thought frustrated the hell out of him, but to his surprise the surge of admiration was stronger.

'But I'm not having sex at your convenience,' she finished. 'I decide when I'm ready, and I'm not ready yet. And until you stop freezing me out every time I ask you a personal question you'd better prepare yourself for a long wait.'

'That's blackmail,' he said, astounded at her gall.

'Call it what you like,' she said, not remotely offended. 'But I'm not comfortable sleeping with a stranger, that's all.'

His heart pounded hard in his chest as he stared at her. Seeing the stubborn line of her jaw and the resolve in her eyes, it dawned on him that she really wasn't going to budge on this. She'd got him again. If he wanted to take this any further he was going to have to give her a little piece of himself. He swallowed heavily, looked away, out into the gardens of Havensmere. The gardens that he'd designed and nurtured for no reason he understood.

Should he risk it? Could he? But then he thought about how much he wanted her. Of how defenceless his child would be if he didn't at least give it his name. And he knew he didn't have much of a choice.

Her fingers touched the bare skin of his forearm and his gaze jerked back to hers.

'Is it really so hard to talk about yourself?' she murmured, the note of sympathy disturbing him more.

Her fingers fell away as he shoved his hand in his pocket. 'Of course not,' he lied. 'If it's that big a deal I don't mind answering your questions.' All he had to do was ensure he didn't tell her too much. 'In fact, I've got a few of my own.'

Information was power, and it was becoming blindingly obvious he didn't know enough about her either, or he wouldn't have underestimated her so drastically again. Why not turn this little heart-to-heart of hers to his advantage?

His confidence finally returning, he mustered a smile. 'I'll make some coffee, and we'll talk out on the terrace,' he said, reconciled to keeping his libido under control for one more night. 'But I want to make one thing clear.' He ran the pad of his thumb down her cheek and felt her tremble as she nodded. His confidence got another satisfying boost. 'Once we've had our little chat there'll be no more evasions. You can have tonight, but after that the gloves are off. Understood?'

She grinned. 'Perfectly,' she said, putting her hands on his shoulders. She lifted up on tiptoe and gave him a quick kiss. 'As long as there are no kinky perversions involved, I'm sure I'll be amenable.' She shot him a coquettish look. 'Very amenable.'

He took her wrist as she turned away. 'Define kinky.'

'Hmm.' She pressed her index finger to her lips. 'Well, spanking for one,' she said, but then paused to rake her teeth over that tempting bottom lip. 'Actually, no—

spanking's probably okay.' She tapped his nose. 'As long as I can spank you back.'

'You cheeky little…'

Luke went to grab her, but missed as she shot out through the terrace doors, her mischievous giggle trailing behind her.

'Spanking's the least of your worries, madam,' he shouted after her. But he had to concede she'd won the round.

CHAPTER FIFTEEN

'BERWICK was my father.' Luke took a sip of his coffee. 'That's how I inherited this place—the title,' he said as he put his cup down on the terrace table.

A slight breeze ruffled Louisa's hair as she stared dumbly at Luke. She could taste the sweet fragrance of the flower gardens on the air. The scent cast a potent spell in the amber glow of the sinking sun, but it wasn't nearly potent enough to distract Louisa from her racing heartbeat. She crossed her legs and tried to even out her breathing.

'Oh, I see,' she said.

She didn't know what else to say. His candour had stunned her. She hadn't really expected him to tell her something so personal. But then, from the indifferent look on his face, she wasn't sure he considered it to be all that personal.

So that was why he had been so upset about her magazine article. He was illegitimate and he didn't want anyone to know about it. But why had he been so determined to keep it a secret? Why did he consider it such a stigma?

'Oh, is right,' he said on a sharp note of bitterness. 'I wasn't too happy when I found out.'

'Why not?' she asked. 'I mean, I know it must have been a bit of a shock when you heard his will and everything.

But…' She looked round at the gardens, the beauty of the house behind them. 'This place is so incredible. Surely you must have been a little bit pleased that he'd left it to you, and that he'd acknowledged you by giving you the title?'

She stumbled to a halt. His jaw had gone rigid. She'd offended him somehow. 'I'm sorry. Obviously this is a sore point. I didn't mean to—'

'On the contrary,' he interrupted her. 'It's not a sore point at all. So there's no need to apologise,' he said nonchalantly, but his jaw was still as hard as granite. Clearly his relationship with his father was a very sore point indeed. 'But I didn't want Havensmere or the title,' he continued. 'I took them in the end because the place was a wreck and restoring it seemed like a good business investment,' he said carefully—so carefully it sounded as if he were trying to convince himself instead of her. 'And I didn't find out Berwick was my father after his death,' he said flatly. 'I found out when my mother died.'

'How old were you?' she asked, afraid to hear the answer.

'Seven,' he said.

The rush of sympathy, of understanding, made tears well in her eyes. 'Luke, I'm so sorry.' She reached across the table and grasped his hand, squeezed. 'I know how awful it is to lose someone you love when you're still a child.'

How telling, she thought, that they should have something so painful in common. But then she noticed he didn't look sad. He looked indifferent.

'How do you know what it feels like?' he asked.

'My mother died, too, when I was in my teens.'

'That's tough.' He reached across, brushed the tears from her cheeks. 'But you don't have to cry for me,' he said awkwardly. 'Luckily I was younger. I don't remember my mother all that well.'

What a strange thing to say. Surely not being able to remember his mother would make the loss harder to bear, not easier?

'How did you find out Berwick was your father?' she asked, as it began to dawn on her why he wanted to save his own child from illegitimacy. How dreadful it must have been for him—a motherless little boy with a father who didn't want him.

Luke could see the compassion in her eyes. Something loosened deep inside him and he stiffened. He didn't want her concern, her understanding. He had to put a stop to this little pity party—and quickly. He'd revealed far too much already.

'She had a will. She named him as my father,' he said abruptly. 'Berwick ordered blood tests to confirm it.'

'But he didn't claim you?'

Luke shrugged, but the movement felt stiff. Just thinking about Berwick made him feel exposed and needy in a way he hadn't since he was a child. 'Berwick brought me to the UK, paid for a respected boarding school. I did okay.'

She didn't need to know he'd hated the place on sight.

The draughty corridors and stodgy food; the endless rain; the scorn of the other boys because he was a bastard and knew nothing about cricket or rugby; the pitying glances of the housemaster and his wife when he had to stay in school during the holidays, because he had nowhere else to go; the desperate, grinding loneliness.

He'd survived it. In fact he'd triumphed over it. In a funny way, now he thought about it, Berwick had done him a favour. Berwick's rejection had made Luke the man he was today. Emotionally self-sufficient, he didn't need anyone and no one needed him. He liked it that way.

'I got a good education,' he said. 'Everything worked out fine.'

'But who looked after you, Luke? Who took care of your emotional needs?'

What emotional needs? he wanted to say, but didn't. This was all getting way too deep, and way too intimate. He'd given her enough—more than enough.

'You've had your questions,' he said. He picked up her hand, brought her fingers to his lips. 'Now I've got one for you.'

'But I—'

He held up his finger to silence her. 'Uh-uh. Fair's fair. You had your turn.'

She huffed out a breath, and he could see she wanted to object but thought better of it. 'All right—fine. I guess a deal's a deal,' she said reluctantly. 'What do you want to know about me?'

'I want to know why you've got such a problem with male authority figures.'

She scowled. 'Like you, you mean?'

'Just answer the question,' he said, toying with her fingers and enjoying her irritation. She really did look ridiculously cute when she was annoyed.

'Well, for starters I don't consider it a problem.'

'You're still not answering the question,' he said. She wasn't getting off the hook that easily.

Her eyes flashed hot, but he could see the flush of awareness too—and felt an answering tug of lust. Okay, maybe it was a little perverse—he'd certainly never felt this way about any other woman—but arguing with her definitely got him hot.

'It's no big secret,' she said. 'My father's a traditional Italian *papà*. I love him to bits, but he thinks it's his God-given right to stick his nose into my business and tell me what to do—just because he's a man and he's my dad. We had what you might call a difficult relationship after my mother died because of it. But we're mostly over it now.'

'Ah-ha,' he said, as if he were Isaac Newton under the apple tree. 'So that explains that huge chip you've got on your shoulder about women's rights.'

'What chip?' She tried to pull her hand out of his. He held fast. 'Let go. I refuse to hold hands with a male chauvinist pig.'

He stood up and hauled her out of her chair. 'What makes you think you have a choice?'

'I most certainly do…'

He wrapped his arms around her, cuffing her wrists behind her back. Trussed like that, her breasts thrust against his chest and the juncture of her thighs cradled his hardness.

'What are you doing?' she gasped, in equal parts outrage and arousal.

'Shut up, Louisa,' he said gently, and silenced her next tirade with his mouth.

She struggled for a moment as he feasted on her lips. But as soon as he felt her melt, felt that killer body moulding to his, he drew back. He bit lightly into that pouty bottom lip, and loved the little shiver she gave. The feel of her, soft and pliant in his arms, was almost more than he could stand. But he had a point to make, and he intended to make it. So he forced himself to let her go and plastered a condescending smile on his face.

'You'd better go to bed, Louisa. You're going to need your sleep—I intend to keep you very busy tomorrow.'

Instead of the defiance he had expected, her lips curved and her eyes sparked with mischief.

'Good point, Devereaux,' she said, her eyes drifting down his frame. 'You best do the same. I don't want to tire you out too soon.'

He might have guessed she wouldn't let him get the last word in.

He chuckled as she left him standing alone on the terrace, the adrenalin coursing through him at the thought of what tomorrow would bring.

Who knew defiance would be such a turn-on?

CHAPTER SIXTEEN

LOUISA scowled at the shadows under her eyes in the bathroom mirror.

'Luke Devereaux, I'm going to murder you,' she muttered.

She'd been awake most of the night, after being plagued by a string of luridly erotic dreams with the gloriously naked Luke Devereaux the star performer in all of them. She was a pregnant lady. She needed her sleep. What had he been thinking of last night stirring her up to the point of insanity?

But then she smiled at her reflection. After the games they'd been playing he couldn't have slept any better than she had. The thought made her feel considerably better.

Walking into the bedroom, she pulled open the drapes, looked out across the gardens and debated her next course of action. As soon as she and Luke saw each other again they would end up tearing each other's clothes off. Not that she minded that. There was only so much torture a woman could take in the cause of sexual equality. But last night had given her a few other things to think about besides her raging hormones, which meant she wasn't quite ready to confront him yet. She decided a long, leisurely walk in the mansion's grounds would give her the time she needed before her hormones completely obliterated all coherent thought.

And the biggest topic for consideration was Luke's revelation last night about his parentage. As she had lain awake in the long hours before dawn, she'd begun to wonder about the child he'd been and the man he'd become. What would it have been like to spend most of your childhood alone, without anyone who really cared about you?

She'd thought of her own childhood. While it had been marred by the tearing pain of her mother's death and her father's over-protectiveness, there had always been the bedrock of love. Strong, consistent, unstinting and totally unconditional.

What must it have been like for Luke to grow up without that support?

Maybe his emotional detachment, his need to be in charge all the time, was actually a defence—a way of coping on his own.

She sighed. Well, he wasn't on his own any more. He was going to be a father in six months' time—and that meant he would have to relinquish some of that cast-iron control and learn how to share his feelings.

She gave a rueful smile as she rummaged around in the wardrobe, where her clothes had appeared yesterday evening as if by magic. On the basis of her experience with Luke so far, she could see it was going to be a sharp learning curve for him—but she was more than woman enough for the job.

She found a pair of low-heeled sandals, and a simple summer dress printed with large rosebuds which clashed spectacularly with the wallpaper.

She put the outfit on, checked her appearance in the

room's cheval mirror and blinked in shock. The dress's bodice, held up by two spindly shoulder straps, was a lot snugger than she remembered it. The linen and Lycra mix strained against her ever-increasing bosom. Pretty soon she'd be giving Dolly Parton a run for her money!

Louisa went back to the wardrobe and rooted out a thin cotton cardigan. It was going to be another scorcher outside, with the sun beating down only a few hours after dawn, but she put the cardigan on anyway. Bumping into Luke with her boobs on display would send out entirely the wrong message.

After having breakfast in her room, Louisa snuck out of the house and set out across the gardens at a healthy pace. Mrs Roberts had given her a bottle of mineral water and a hand-drawn map with directions to an old water mill which bordered a lake. The housekeeper had estimated it would take her about two hours to get there and back, which suited Louisa's purposes perfectly. She didn't want Luke thinking she was his for the taking—even if she was.

Ten minutes into the woods, Louisa stopped to see how far she'd come. Her heart lifted as she noticed the astonishing picture Havensmere made behind her, framed against the forest shadows. The flowers planted out front blended together in a rainbow of colours that softened the austere stonework.

Luke really had done an incredible job with the garden design. She made a humming sound of consideration in her throat, which echoed against the ancient woods. How funny that he'd convinced himself he hated Havensmere when it seemed obvious that the opposite was true.

She turned back to the path to trudge on—and stopped dead. Oh, my goodness. She shot round again, stared at the house. Of course—it was so obvious. She felt like Donald Duck with a cartoon lightbulb beaming over her head.

Luke was making a home here—and he didn't even know it. The thought was tantalising, and yet so sweet her heart swelled.

As she walked on, hearing the hum of insects, feeling the sun beating warm against her skin and smelling the fresh, earthy country air, she couldn't force the silly grin off her face. She spotted the lake across an overgrown meadow and struck out towards it, feeling like a child skipping off to the sweetshop. As the long grasses brushed her calves, and sweat trickled down between her breasts, wonderful pictures projected like a rose-tinted home movie in her mind. Luke and her and their beautiful toddler—its wavy brown hair falling in front of clear grey eyes— playing on the lawn, or swimming in the pool, or picking wildflowers together in the shadow of the magnificent house that had made its final transformation into a warm and loving home.

She paused, tried to get a grip—after all, Luke had a long way to go before he was going to be ideal husband and father material—but the daydreams were irresistible. On such a bright, beautiful day, positively brimming with promise, it wasn't hard to believe that their relationship might be at a new and exciting crossroads. She'd certainly enjoyed his company last night—and she'd discovered that there was much more to him than she ever would have expected.

At last she approached the comforting shadows of the abandoned water mill. The derelict building stood stately and silent in the still summer air, its crumbling drystone walls overgrown with weeds and wildflowers. She recognised poppies and bullrushes and a rambling rosebush. The thought that if Luke were with her he could probably tell her the names of the other flowers had her heart giving another little leap.

Peeling off the cardigan now clinging to her skin, she tied it round her waist and reached down to pluck one of the poppies—and she caught the sound of splashing coming from behind the mill.

Someone was swimming in the lake.

As the rhythmic strokes got louder, she edged closer to the mill wall and crouched down. She would look ridiculous if anyone caught her hiding, but she didn't feel like having to explain her presence to one of Luke's groundsmen, or gamekeepers, or whoever it was.

The splashes stopped, and Louisa let out a careful breath. She eased off her knees and shook out her legs. The blood coursed back into her numb ankles, making her wince.

She froze as a dark head appeared out of the water fifteen feet away. Strong hands gripped the worm-eaten wood of the old dock on the opposite bank. The misshapen planks creaked as the swimmer surged out of the water in one smooth, fluid manoeuvre. Louisa had to slap a hand over her mouth to contain the gasp as he stood on the dock, his back to her, all sleek, tanned flesh and muscled sinews, water glistening on his naked skin. She would have recognised that upright, arrogant stance anywhere—even though Luke Devereaux didn't have a stitch on.

He walked with an easy predatory grace, his footfalls silent, and bent to pick up the towel beside a pile of clothes. Louisa's eyes dropped to the paler skin of his backside. Firm, beautifully shaped buttocks flexed at the top of long, lean flanks sprinkled with dark hair. She swallowed heavily. No question about it. Her dreams last night had not done that butt justice.

Louisa sucked in a breath as he rubbed the towel across his torso and over his head. What on earth was she supposed to do now? He'd hear her if she tried to leave, and anyway she was fast becoming transfixed. He turned slightly and she got a glimpse of his profile before he began to dry his legs in rough, cursory strokes. He looked magnificent. Like the statue of a Greek god. Her eyes followed his movements as he casually rubbed the towel over his private parts. She blinked, stared, her mouth dropping open. Okay, Louisa would hazard a guess no Greek sculptor had ever used Luke Devereaux in the buff as a model. The proportions were all wrong. Her heart pounded so hard she was astonished he couldn't hear the thud.

He wrapped the towel around his hips, hiding his spectacular assets from view, and a strangled groan of protest escaped before she could stop it. His head whipped round, and magnetic silver-grey eyes locked on her face.

Every single part of her began to pulse in time with her deafening heartbeat.

A tantalisingly slow smile lifted one corner of his mouth. The potent mix of amusement and arousal heating his gaze detonated a nuclear reaction in her nerve endings.

'Hello, Louisa,' he said, as if he were at a church social and she hadn't just been ogling every naked inch of him.

The dam of sensations broke inside her, and surged through her body.

'You were swimming naked,' she blurted out, and felt like an idiot.

He stepped off the dock. She stumbled back, her retreat halted by the rough stone of the mill. Erotic fantasies were one thing. Having them come true was quite another, she discovered.

Talk about being caught between a rock and a hard place.

'I was cooling off after my jog,' he said. He stopped in

front of her, so close her eyes were level with the wisps of wet hair flattened against his chest. 'Or rather I was until you got here.'

Her eyes inched down the arrow of hair which led past the ridged muscles of his abdomen and dwindled to a fine line to bisect his belly button. She gulped, trying to ease the dryness in her throat, as her eyes darted back to his.

God, he was more gorgeous naked than she could possibly have imagined.

His lips quirked. 'Look all you want, Louisa.' He tilted his head to one side, his gaze drifting down to her breasts. 'But in the interests of fair play…' His eyes moved back to her face, the steely-grey challenging her. 'I say we even things out.'

She coughed, gave a half-laugh, scouring her mind for a pithy retort. 'Who says I want to play fair,' she croaked, the thin bodice of her dress so confining it might as well have been a whalebone corset.

'Well, then, I guess I'm going to have to persuade you,' he said, bracing one hand above her head. He lifted the other and trailed his thumb under her chin. The soft pad traced down her neck, leaving a trail of fire in its wake, then pressed against the hammer thuds of her pulse.

'You look hot,' he said.

She swallowed. *You don't say.*

'And the water's incredibly…' His lips lifted in a devilish smile. 'Stimulating.'

She quivered, her nipples pebbling into hard points. 'Stimulating is good,' she said.

His hand spanned her collarbone, his index finger easing under the strap of her dress. Her breath hitched.

'But if I'm going to get naked,' she rasped, 'I can think of something I'd rather do than go swimming.'

'Can you really?' His eyes sharpened as his cool fingers continued to tease the swell of her cleavage where swollen flesh strained.

Her breath panted out as he cupped the underside of her breast and lifted, as if testing its new weight. His thumb rubbed the peak, backwards and forwards. Shock waves of sensation shimmered through her and a staggered groan escaped.

He leaned close, drops of water from his hair dampening the stretched fabric of her bodice. 'Just so you know,' he murmured as he angled his head and his breath feathered across her cheek, 'once we start, I'm not going to stop. So you'd better be ready this time.'

His lips felt deliciously cool but far from soothing as he kissed her neck, licked at the pulse-point.

'Luke,' she groaned, her head falling back to give him better access, her fingers clutching the smooth velvet flesh of his waist. 'Just so *you* know.' She slid her thumbs under the towel, felt him shudder. 'If you start and then stop I'll have to murder you in your sleep.'

He chuckled, pushing the straps of the dress off her shoulders. 'Sounds like we've finally found something we can agree on.'

She drew back, holding up the drooping bodice as she clung to a final thin thread of sanity. 'Except we can't stay here.' She choked out the words. 'What if someone sees us?'

He took her wrists, pulled her arms down to her sides as his lips continued to torment the soft skin of her neck. 'There's no one here but the two of us, I promise,' he whispered.

His lips teased the corner of her mouth, then his tongue demanded entry. All thoughts of propriety were obliterated in a blast of pure animal lust as she sank into the kiss.

Having wild, uninhibited open-air sex with this man in a meadow full of wildflowers might be impossibly reckless, but it felt absolutely right.

She shuddered as his palm swept up her leg, bunching the fabric of her dress. He found the gusset of her knickers and she pressed herself wantonly into his palm.

'You've got too many clothes on,' he muttered, pulling her arms from around his neck so he could push the bodice of her dress down.

She helped him, struggling out of the confining garment, not caring any more if the whole world could see them. She wanted his hands on her. She wanted to explore every glorious inch of him.

He yanked the damp towel off and laid it on the grass. She stared down at him. He was already fully erect—and the sight was both magnificent and intimidating. She felt the throbbing at her core. He lay on the towel, dragged her down, co-cooning their bodies in the tall spray of meadow flowers.

'You're still overdressed,' he murmured, stripping off her knickers.

The matching bra followed moments later, her breath heaving out as her breasts were freed from the restricting lace. The light summer breeze tickled her naked flesh.

His fingers traced the red marks where her bra cups had dug in. 'You need a bigger size,' he said, his eyes turbulent with emotion as they met hers. 'Let's kiss it better.'

Oh, yes, please.

She plunged shaking fingers through his damp hair as his tongue slid across the reddened flesh. Her breath gushed out as he took one puckered nipple into his mouth and bit it lightly. Raw heat flooded between her thighs. She clamped her legs together, trying to hold the inferno back as he worked the same magic on her other breast.

He smoothed his hand down her abdomen, stroked where the baby grew. 'Pregnancy suits you,' he said. 'I may have to keep you this way for the rest of our lives.'

The possessive statement made her heart jolt. What did that mean? But then his hand strayed lower and she couldn't breathe any more, let alone think.

'Open your legs,' he coaxed, probing the silky curls of her sex. Again she obeyed him without complaint, holding him as he drew his thumb down, brushed over her clitoris. She bucked wildly at the tiny touch. Incredible—how could she be so close to orgasm so soon? One more touch and she would surely be there. But he didn't give her the touch she yearned for.

Holding her hips, he angled her pelvis, positioned himself above her, then thrust slowly, solidly until his penis was lodged hard inside her. She moaned, her hands gripping his shoulders as the full, brutally stretched feeling had her pleasure fading.

'It's too much,' she said, straining against the shocking invasion.

He gave her a fleeting kiss. 'Give it a moment,' he said, with all the arrogance of a man in total control.

'In my fantasies you were a lot more amenable,' she grumbled.

He laughed, but she could hear the tension in his voice, knew he was holding back, waiting for her to adjust. She drew her hands down his back. She loved the feel of him, the smooth silk of naked flesh, the firmness of bunched muscles beneath.

Sliding one hand under her bottom, he began to move. The small, rocking motions sent tiny licks of pleasure through her and the discomfort faded. She moved with him, tried to match his rhythm, but she knew she was a long way from the glorious release promised moments before.

'That feels nice,' she said. 'If you can keep it up for an hour it might work.'

He laughed, but the sound was harsh. 'Give her a couple of orgasms and suddenly she's a damn critic. Couldn't you just fake it?' he teased.

'Forget it. I'm never doing that again,' she said, knowing that with him she would never have to.

'Let's try a different position,' he said. 'We haven't found what I was looking for.' He pulled her leg high over his hip and rolled onto his back, taking her with him. Suddenly she was straddling him, and he was impossibly deep. He grunted as her muscles clenched, struggling to adapt to this new, overwhelming sensation. Then he flexed his hips and nudged a place deep inside her.

She cried out, her body raked by a wave of pure pleasure so intense she thought she might faint.

'That's more like it,' he growled. He held her hips, bucked under her, going deeper still, and the rush of orgasm intensified. Then he reached down, exposed the nub of her clitoris with his thumb and rubbed. One small stroke, one hard thrust, and she crashed over the edge, crying out as the tidal wave of sensation hurtled through her.

She sobbed, tried to catch her breath as his fingers dug into her hips. He held on, pumping into her and forcing her into the grip of another titanic orgasm. She tumbled into oblivion, her body collapsing on top of his in a quivering mass—and heard him shout out her name as he emptied inside her.

She could hear the buzz of insects and the staggered rise and fall of his breathing. His chest hair tickled her cheek as the final waves of orgasm shimmered through her body.

She'd never felt more exhausted or more exhilarated in her entire life. She had thought he'd already shown her what sex could be, but their first night didn't even come close to what she'd just experienced.

Gentle fingers brushed the hair from her face, slid down her back to stroke. His hands cupped her bottom and caressed.

'How did that rate with your fantasy, then?' he asked, his voice gruff and a tad self-satisfied.

'Mmm,' she said, using every last ounce of her strength to lift her head. Bracing her hands in the soft grass on either side of him, she studied him in the dreamy shadows cast by the mill. Framed by wildflowers, the strong angles and planes of his face looked outrageously handsome.

Prince Charming eat your heart out.

She ran her finger down his nose. 'You'll have to do it again for me to rate it properly.'

He nipped her fingertip, grinned. 'You little tease,' he said. His hands roamed up her spine, pulled her back down until she was snuggled against his chest. 'We're liable to kill ourselves if we do that again too soon.'

She giggled, listening to the insistent beat of his heart as his lips nuzzled her hair and his thumbs traced the ridge of her spine.

And, just like that, she felt her heart tumble into love.

Her eyes snapped open.

Don't be ridiculous. She couldn't possibly be in love with him. It would put her at too much of a disadvantage. That sudden swooping feeling in her chest a moment ago hadn't been love. It couldn't be. It was just endorphins. She was doing that dumb thing of mistaking sex for love again, that was all. Her heartbeat finally began to slow, to even out.

A firm slap on her rump brought her sharply back to reality. 'Ow!'

'No falling asleep on top of me.' Luke's voice rumbled out, not sounding all that lover-like. He rolled her off him and stood up, then reached down and hauled her up beside him.

'Let's freshen up in the lake,' he said, massaging her shoulders as he gave her a quick peck on the forehead. 'Then we can head back to the house.' He took her hand, marched towards the dock. 'So far we've made love against a wall and in a field. It's about bloody time we got to a bed.'

He'd led her halfway down the dock before her mind cleared enough to register his intent.

She dug her heels into the warm wood. 'No way. I'm not going in the lake,' she said, with as much dignity as she could muster while she was stark naked in a field and still rosy with afterglow.

He stepped back to her and hefted her easily into his arms.

'Put me down,' she squealed, kicking her legs and wriggling furiously. 'It's probably freezing.'

He kept striding down the dock. 'It's warm. The water's not that deep.'

'But I'm with child,' she squeaked, struggling in earnest now. 'The shock might harm the baby.'

'Rubbish—the baby will be fine. It's as healthy as you are,' he said, and walked right off the end of the dock.

She shrieked as they hit the water together—forgot to close her mouth as they plunged beneath the surface, and swallowed half the lake.

CHAPTER SEVENTEEN

'Come on, Sleeping Beauty, time to wake up. Breakfast's here,' Luke murmured, his lips nuzzling Louisa's nape.

'Go away, I'm asleep,' Louisa grumbled. She kept her eyes firmly closed and snuggled into the pillow, enjoying the fresh scent of the fine linen sheets, the pleasant ache from their morning lovemaking and the last vestiges of a very erotic dream.

'Don't make me do this the hard way.' His breath brushed her earlobe, sending a shiver of awareness through her bloodstream.

'Shoo.' She tried to flick him away, her eyes still shut.

'The hard way it is, then.'

The mattress dipped, and her eyes flew open as she was hoisted up in strong arms. She grappled to pull the sheet over her nakedness and push the tangle of hair out of her eyes as he marched across the room. 'This won't do you any good. I'm not hungry.'

'Rubbish—you're starving. You always are,' he said, laughing, as he placed her in a chair.

'I'm not eating breakfast in the nude.' She wriggled round, hoisting the sheet up, and got ready to bolt back to bed.

'Oh, yes, you are,' he replied, a wicked grin on his face as he lifted the domed cover off her plate.

She sagged back into the seat. The salty aroma of bacon wafted up as she gazed longingly at the full English breakfast. Fluffy scrambled eggs, Cumberland sausage, grilled tomatoes, mushrooms in cream and—*the pièce de resistance*—two rashers of crisp streaky bacon.

Her stomach rumbled. 'That's cheating,' she moaned.

'Tough,' he said, placing a knife and fork beside her plate.

She scowled at him as he poured her a glass of freshly squeezed orange juice. He looked disgustingly awake, wearing a newly ironed pair of chinos and a T-shirt, and with his dark wavy hair still damp from his shower. She muttered something derogatory, but wrapped the sheet round her breasts and tucked the end down her cleavage.

'Don't be such a sore loser,' he said, whipping back the drapes beside the table. Mid-morning sunlight streamed into the room, clearing the sleep from her brain.

Louisa's heart stuttered as she took in his striking face, gilded by the sun. Goodness, but the man had more than his fair share of blessings from the good-looks fairies. With those sensual lips, the chiselled cheeks and the hint of stubble shadowing his jaw he looked irresistible.

She felt the familiar swooping drop in her chest that had been plaguing her for three whole days—ever since their tryst by the lake. In the long lazy summer days since they'd argued about everything from party politics to which side of the bed to sleep on, flirted with each other mercilessly, scored points off each other every chance they got, and made wild passionate love too many times to count. And she'd adored every minute of it. She picked up her fork and smiled to herself. There didn't seem much point in denying it any longer.

She was hopelessly in love with this devastating man.

He sat opposite her, glanced up and frowned.

'Eat,' he ordered, nodding at her plate. 'Before it gets cold.'

Or rather she was hopelessly in love with this domineering tyrant.

'All right already,' she said, putting on a terrible New York accent, and shovelled some scrambled eggs on to her fork. 'Keep your hair on.'

Okay, so she'd been an idiot and fallen in love with him again. But at least she was exceptionally well aware of his faults now. He wasn't the charmingly romantic Prince Charming she'd met that first night, but a flesh-and-blood man with a stubborn streak a mile wide, a serious problem with relinquishing control and the arrogance to match. Living with Luke would always be a challenge, but in the last three days she had discovered that beneath that tough, take-no-prisoners exterior was a man who had a fierce sense of responsibility, a playful sense of humour, and who was the most generous of lovers. And, luckily for her, she was no pushover.

And anyway, she didn't have to be frightened of her feelings because she had a foolproof plan. She had no intention of throwing herself on his mercy. She would wait for him to declare his love first. And she was positive he was halfway there already. In the last few days he'd shown her in so many subtle ways that he cared about her, that he needed her.

Why else would he bring her breakfast in bed every morning? Why else would he drone on about whether she was looking after herself properly? Why else would he take her on a tour of the gardens, his fingers squeezing hers and his voice thick with pride as he pointed out the careful blend of colours and textures he'd designed? Why else would he make love to her with such urgency, such intensity—as if each time were their last? And why else did he hold her afterwards as if she were the only person who mattered?

She knew he had no idea what was happening to him, and that because of all those defence mechanisms he'd acquired during his childhood it was going to take him a while to figure it out. But she could be patient—especially when the wait was this much fun.

There was only one small fly in the ointment. Apart from their marriage, he didn't seem to want to talk about the future, or about the baby. But she wasn't too worried about it. Lots of men never talked about their feelings unless you pressed them.

She watched him dig into his breakfast as she lifted a piece of granary toast from its wire rack. Now she knew how much she loved him, it was probably about time she started pressing.

'You know, Luke,' she said, brandishing the butter knife, 'you're really going to have to learn to curb your caveman tendencies before our daughter arrives, or there's likely to be trouble. Little girls don't respond well to being ordered about by their fathers. Believe me I know,' she quipped.

She waited for him to rise to the bait, but instead he went still. 'You survived,' he said, but the relaxed humour of a moment ago had disappeared.

Louisa frowned. 'Only after my father learned to—'

'Can we talk about something else?' he interrupted, his eyes meeting hers at last.

She put the toast down. That hadn't quite gone according to plan. She'd mentioned the baby yesterday and he'd subtly changed the subject. He hadn't even been subtle this time.

Clearly pressing him wasn't going to be enough. 'Why don't you want to talk about the baby?' she asked bluntly.

He stopped cutting his sausage. 'It's not due for six

months. There's nothing to talk about.' He gave her an exasperated look. 'Except when you plan to marry me, and you're the one who won't talk about *that*.'

She felt the fanciful little leap that always accompanied the topic of his marriage proposal, but forced it down. She knew a diversionary tactic when she saw one. 'I've told you why I won't discuss marrying you. It's far too soon.' *Maybe when you've got the guts to tell me how you really feel about me, then I'll discuss marriage.* 'And there are tons of things to discuss about the baby.'

His eyebrow lifted. 'Like what?'

Why was he being deliberately obtuse?

'Well…' She grasped for the most obvious examples. 'How about possible names? What should we call it? A child's name is very important, and—'

'I don't have a preference. Whatever you decide I'm sure I'll be fine with it,' he said, so dismissively her apprehension increased. 'As long as it's not Elvis.'

He was trying to be funny. They'd argued yesterday about whether Elvis was really the King of Rock 'n' Roll. But now Louisa had never felt less like laughing.

'What about antenatal classes, then?' she asked. 'And do you want to be there at the birth?'

He put his knife and fork down. 'I don't know,' he said carefully. But she could see the answer in his eyes—and it was no.

'Luke, you're starting to scare me. Do you have a problem with the baby?'

Luke swallowed, struggling to ignore his impatience and the flicker of guilt underneath. Why did they need to talk about this *now*? Why was she forcing the issue?

Everything had been going so well since their morning

at the lake. She'd proved to be a better match for him than any woman he'd ever dated. Her irreverent wit and lively intelligence made her an entertaining opponent in any argument, and he'd laughed more in the last few days than he had since he was a child. And the sex was incredible—more satisfying, more fulfilling than anything he'd ever experienced before. He was a demanding lover, but she'd met all his demands with demands of her own, and he hadn't tired of her yet—not even close. But he couldn't let her or the child come to mean too much to him. He knew what it was like to be dependent on others—and he never intended to expose himself to that kind of misery again.

He lifted her hand, which had fisted on the table, eased the palm open. 'Louisa—relax, sweetheart. Of course I don't have a problem with the baby.' He'd offered to marry her, hadn't he? How much more involved did she want him to be? 'I just don't think I'll be any good at the day-to-day stuff,' he said cautiously. 'I'm sure you'll handle it fine without me.'

'Without you?' she asked dumbly.

She didn't look wary any more. She looked horrified.

Luke ruthlessly controlled the urge to take the words back, to apologise.

Their relationship had limits and this was one of them—she needed to understand that. But why did the thought of telling her the truth make him suddenly feel so hollow?

He struggled to regain the feeling of certainty, of invulnerability that had always sustained him in the past. He had to start setting some parameters to their relationship before this got any more complicated.

'I'm sure you'll make a great mother, Louisa. You won't need me there,' he said, but the words were much harder to say than he'd expected.

* * *

Louisa stared at Luke, the warmth of the sun on her bare shoulders doing nothing to ease the chill around her heart. The hearty breakfast she'd been eating churned inside her. He couldn't mean it, surely? That he intended to have no real role in their child's life?

But his face had gone blank. He looked so closed-off, so controlled, she barely recognised him. Where was the man who had held her so tenderly, who had teased her and made her laugh, who had made love to her with such passion—and who had spent a small fortune turning Havensmere into a home?

Where was the man she loved? The man she had simply assumed would love their child.

'Of course I'll need you there,' she said, the words sounding dull and unreal. Why was she having to explain this to him? 'How can you say that? You asked me to marry you, Luke. Why would you do that if you don't want to take any real part in our child's life?'

'I don't see what the problem is,' he said, his tone stiff and defensive.

'But if we got married we'd be living together. How could you just ignore your baby?' She could hear the desperation in her voice and hated it, but what choice did she have? Surely he could see that what he was suggesting was madness?

He seemed to consider that for a moment. 'I see your point,' he said, but as she sighed with relief he continued in the same toneless voice. 'Living together in the long term probably wouldn't work.'

His thumb brushed the back of her hand, but she hardly felt it.

'I'd want to visit you, of course,' he said. 'And I plan to buy you a place more suitable for you and the baby. But if I moved in, you're right—it would probably confuse things. Especially once the baby's born.'

'Confuse things…?' Her fingers had gone numb, and she pulled them out of his grasp. She folded her arms across her chest, tucked her hands under her armpits, suddenly feeling desperately exposed. He didn't want to live with them? She could hardly grasp the reality of what he was implying. Had she really made such a terrible mistake? Had she really misread his intentions towards her and her child so completely?

'You want to make me your mistress?' she said dully.

'How could you be my mistress if we're married?' he said, sounding annoyed.

'Why do you want to marry me at all?' she asked, tears pricking her eyes. 'If you don't want to live with me or with our child?' A lone tear spilled over her eyelid.

'Louisa, for heaven's sake, why are you crying? You *know* why I asked you to marry me. I don't want my child to be illegitimate.'

She gulped down the sob that wanted to burst out, pressed her fingers to her lips. She'd been a complete fool. He didn't love her at all. But, much worse than that, he didn't want to love their child either.

She gathered the sheet up, forced herself out of the chair, the lancing pain in her heart almost more than she could bear. 'I have to go home,' she stammered as she rushed towards the bathroom.

She'd taken less than two steps before he spun her round. 'What's the matter with you?'

'Don't touch me,' she snapped at him, trying to muster her temper to hide the hurt.

'Okay,' he said, lifting his hands as if he'd touched a live flame. 'I won't touch you as long as you tell me why you look so devastated. Surely you can see this is the best solution for everyone concerned?'

She swiped the tears from her cheeks, determined not to let him see her crack. She had her pride. Right now it was all she had. And then another horrifying thought occurred to her, and her knees began to tremble.

'Why did you sleep with me, Luke? Just answer me that.'

His brows drew together. 'You know perfectly well why.'

'Actually, no, I don't.' She dragged the sheet round her, held it tight and locked her knees to stop herself collapsing in a heap. 'Was it because you wanted me, or because you thought it was a good way to coerce me into this sham of a marriage you have planned?'

'I don't know what you mean,' he said, but she saw the flicker of alarm before he could mask it. 'Our marriage will be legally binding.' He took her arm, hauled her towards him. 'And I intend to exercise every one of my conjugal rights—so it won't be a sham.'

She wrestled herself away from him. 'Of course it will be a sham. How could it be anything else if we don't love each other? If we don't have a future together?'

For a moment he looked as if she'd slapped him. But then he gave a toneless laugh.

'What has *love* got to do with anything?' he said, his eyes so bleak she shivered. 'What we're talking about here is an unplanned pregnancy and two people with a strong sexual attraction to each other. I'm not looking for love, and neither are you.'

She rubbed her arms to stave off the cold, felt all her hopes and dreams crumble to dust. 'Unfortunately that's where you're wrong. I am looking for love.' More tears streamed down her cheeks, but this time she didn't bother to wipe them away. 'It was all just a game to you, wasn't it?' she said, seeing it all so clearly. He'd used her feelings against her, her romantic heart, and she'd let him. The anger drained away to leave a great gaping hole of pity—for them both. 'You always have to win, don't you, Luke? By whatever means necessary.'

Luke struggled to hold down the unreasoning rush of fear at the sadness in her voice. 'That's not true,' he said, his voice breaking. He cleared his throat, tried again. 'I never pretended I wanted more. I never said that. I played fair with you. You're the one trying to turn this into something it isn't.' The words sounded false even to him.

'You're right,' she said, the resignation in her voice making his panic increase. 'You never said you wanted more. I suppose you did play fair. But the problem is I stopped playing days ago, when I made the stupid mistake of falling in love with you.'

He recoiled from the words instinctively. She wasn't the first woman to tell him she loved him. But something twisted deep inside him—and all the platitudes he'd used in the past to deal with unwanted declarations of love wouldn't come. He should point out that love didn't mean anything to him. That he didn't need it. That he'd made damn sure he would never need it. But the denial got trapped behind the lump that had come from nowhere and got stuck in his throat.

'You know what's really ironic?' she whispered. 'You kept playing and you didn't even know you'd already won.'

The quiet acceptance that was so unlike her made the something twist even harder inside him as he watched her walk away. She should have looked foolish, with the sheet trailing behind her, but she held herself with the regal stature of Cleopatra on her barge, her shoulderblades so rigid with dignity they stood out starkly against the smooth line of her naked back.

'I'll take a cab to the station,' she said without turning round. 'It's better if we don't see each other again.'

Panic closed his throat as the bathroom door banged shut and he heard the lock click into place.

The sound reverberated in his mind and a desperate longing welled up inside him. He took two steps forward. He couldn't let her go. He wanted her to stay. But the desperation brought with it a bitter flash of memory that stopped him in his tracks and whisked him back to the worst moment of his childhood.

He sat scared and silent in Berwick's study, his sneakered feet dangling down, sweat staining his Spiderman T-shirt. *Please let him want me*, came the childish whisper in his mind, but then Berwick shouted, 'Look at me, boy,' and his head jerked up to see the frigid contempt in his father's cold grey eyes.

Luke cut the memory off, determined not to let the crushing feeling of worthlessness engulf him all over again. Anger surged through him, obliterating the pain. How dare she do this to him? How dare she make him feel things he didn't want to feel—need things he didn't want to need?

He stormed across the room, thumped the door with a clenched fist. 'You're not going anywhere,' he shouted through the bathroom door. No reply. 'I'll give you time to get dressed and then you can come to my study so we can discuss this properly.'

He couldn't confront her now. He might do something he'd regret. But she wasn't going to get away with this. She was asking him for things he didn't want to give her. None of this was his fault. She was the one who had moved the goalposts, not him.

Which meant *she* was the one who would have to learn to deal with it.

Louisa collapsed against the bathroom door, felt the brutal thuds as Luke's fist hit the other side and heard his shouted demands. She clasped her hands round her knees and realised she was back where she'd started three months ago, when she had first fallen in love with him. But this time she bit back the wrenching sobs as she heard his footsteps fade away.

She covered her belly with trembling hands, stroked.

'Don't worry,' she whispered to her unborn child. 'He might not love you, but I'll make sure I love you enough for both of us.'

CHAPTER EIGHTEEN

LUKE shoved the squash racquet into his locker and slammed the door shut.

'Hey, buddy, don't take it so hard,' came Jack's relaxed voice as he entered the locker room of the exclusive Mayfair sports club. 'You can't win 'em all.'

Yeah, but he hadn't won a match in two solid weeks.

'You're just off your game,' Jack finished, sitting on the bench and untying his squash shoes.

Luke took a steadying breath, rubbed the knotted muscles at the top of his spine. He had to calm down. He was behaving like a two-year-old having a tantrum. Jack would think he'd gone mad. He flushed, recalling his surly behaviour on the court.

'I've behaved like an ass today, Jack,' he said, pasting a tight smile on his face. 'I apologise.'

He pulled his sweat-sodden shirt over his head and stuffed it in his gym bag. A headache of epic proportions hammered away at his temples.

The truth was, it wasn't just his form on the squash court that had deserted him in the last two weeks. He hadn't been sleeping properly, he felt distracted all the time—and he hadn't even been able to keep his mind on his business affairs. He'd made a rookie's mistake yesterday, and watched helpless as close to two hundred thousand pounds had been wiped off his share value in the space of five minutes.

Jack looked up, wrapping a towel round his hips. 'No sweat,' he said. 'You want to grab some lunch once we're done here?'

'Sure,' Luke said. Then felt pathetic as he watched Jack disappear into the shower room. He'd be terrible company, but the rest of the afternoon and evening stretched out before him like an endurance test. Since when had he found it so hard to tolerate his own company?

He sat on the bench, tugged off his shoes and threw them into his bag on top of the shirt.

He knew exactly when it had happened. When Louisa DiMarco had swept into his life like a hurricane, wreaked havoc, and then left him to pick up the pieces. The woman was a bona fide natural disaster area. He hoped she was pleased with herself.

He still couldn't believe she'd run out on him. So much for her being in love with him, as she'd claimed. If she loved him she'd have come to his study as he'd asked. She wouldn't have sneaked out of Havensmere that morning two weeks ago without even saying goodbye.

The fury that had gripped him ever since he'd discovered her gone made his hands clumsy as he peeled off the rest of his clothes and slung a towel round his hips.

The woman had so much to answer for it wasn't even funny.

The minute Mrs Roberts had told him about her departure he'd raced down to the garage to follow her in the car. But he'd thought better of driving to the train station and dragging her back once he'd got in.

Why should he chase after her? She was the one who'd

got some stupid bee in her bonnet about love. She was the one who had to come to her senses. He'd done the decent, the responsible thing by offering to marry her and support their child. She'd as good as thrown his offer back in his face by running off like that.

But as the days had passed and she hadn't even called the impotent rage had increased. She was a reckless, irresponsible fool. She needed him. Why couldn't she see that?

How was she going to cope in that tiny flat? What was she going to do for money once the baby was born? He didn't want his child growing up in squalor. The whole situation was completely intolerable. Why should he have to make a commitment he wasn't comfortable with?

He stomped into the shower room, ducked into one of the cubicles and turned on the unit full blast. The frigid water hit him in the face.

He could hear Jack singing some old Motown tune in the cubicle next door. Jack always sang in the shower. It used to amuse Luke—how could a guy be as happy as Jack when he had so many burdens, so many people relying on him?

But as Luke felt the water warm up, and listened to Jack's deep voice crooning something about sitting on the dock of a bay, he didn't find his friend's singing funny any more.

Jack had his plump, pretty wife Mel to go home to tonight. Jack had that tank-like toddler who would cling to his neck when he picked him up. And Jack had that little girl with the bright blue eyes who would run at him full pelt, wrap her arms round his legs and call him Daddy as soon as he walked through the door.

And what did Luke have?

He had his solitude. That was what he had. Luke had his independence and his pride and his self-control. But somehow the sense of well-being, the satisfaction that had always accompanied that thought, wouldn't come any more. Because Luke only had a lonely penthouse to go home to, and a palatial country estate that felt unbearably empty now without Louisa there.

Steam fogged up the cubicle as Luke shampooed his hair and slicked the sweat off his body with the complimentary toiletries. He let the water pummel his tired, aching muscles and felt the anger, the fury, the rage that had sustained him for the last two weeks wash down the drain with the shampoo foam.

He gave a weary sigh and turned off the shower control. Just as he had feared, the traitorous feelings lurking beneath—of regret, inadequacy and loneliness—hadn't been washed away as well, but festered inside him. This was all Louisa's fault too, he thought bitterly.

When he walked into the locker room Jack was combing his hair, already dressed.

His friend scowled. 'You look like hell, man.'

Luke dumped his towel and pulled on a clean pair of boxers. 'Cheers,' he said wryly. You could always rely on Jack to tell it like it was.

He hadn't felt this isolated and confused since he was seven years old and a policeman had turned up at his babysitter's apartment to tell him he would never be able to see his mother again. Never feel her arms holding him tight, hear her whisper 'You're my best boy' or smell the peppermint Lifesavers she'd loved to suck on her breath.

It figured he wouldn't be looking his best.

'You want to talk about it?'

Luke looked up from buttoning his shirt to see Jack watching him, a concerned frown wrinkling his brow.

'I'm fine.' The words came out on autopilot. He didn't

have that kind of friendship with Jack. In fact he didn't have that kind of friendship with anyone. Talking about his feelings made him feel weak—just like thinking about his mother did.

Another little shaft of pain and resentment pierced his heart. Louisa had made him talk about his feelings and then she'd run out on him—which just went to show how pointless the whole exercise was. And now he couldn't stop thinking about her—or his mother.

Luke scooped his damp hair back from his brow and refused to give in to the urge to confide in Jack.

'Your foul mood hasn't got anything to do with Louisa's scan today, has it?'

Luke's head shot up. Jack was still looking at him, compassion shadowing his blue eyes. He didn't know what Jack was talking about, so why had his insides turned to putty?

Jack patted him on the shoulder. 'Don't sweat it, buddy. Mel and I had a similar scare when she was pregnant with Cal. Happens all the time. It'll almost certainly turn out to be nothing.' Jack gave him a searching look. 'Although I'm kind of surprised you didn't want to be there with Louisa, seeing as you're obviously as worried about this as she is.'

Luke debated for a few seconds playing along with Jack, pretending he knew what was going on. But the fingers of dread clawing up his throat made him realise he'd never be able to pull it off. 'What scare?' he said, barely able to get the words out.

'You don't know about it?' Jack sounded astonished.

'No, I don't,' he said, pushing back the niggling feeling of guilt. It wasn't his fault Louisa had shut him out. 'What the hell's the scan for?'

'Louisa had an antenatal appointment yesterday at her GP's office. They couldn't find a heartbeat.'

Every last molecule of blood drained out of Luke's head and slammed straight into his heart, making the organ beat so hard he thought it might burst. 'Something's wrong with the baby?' he rasped, panic constricting his airways.

'Calm down, man. Let me explain.' The reasonable tone of his friend's voice and the reassuring weight of the hand on his shoulder did nothing to ease the rapid gunshots of Luke's heartbeat. 'Louisa's GP said their foetal heart monitor's been acting up for weeks. They referred Louisa to the hospital for a scan, just to confirm everything's okay. The GP's not worried, so you don't need to be.'

Luke grabbed his shoes, scrambled to put them on. He fumbled with the laces, his fingers so numb they might have belonged to someone else. 'Which hospital? What time's the scan?'

'UCH,' Jack said. 'And I think the appointment's this afternoon. I'm not exactly sure when.'

'Can you ring Mel? Does she know?' Luke asked, ready to beg if he had to.

'Probably,' Jack replied. 'I'll see what I can find out.' He pulled his mobile phone out of his pocket, keyed in a number.

It took Jack five agonising minutes to finesse Louisa's appointment time out of his wife.

Luke finished getting dressed in a matter of seconds and began pacing the locker room while he waited, resentment and panic turning to a slow-burning anger. Something could be wrong with their child and she hadn't told him. Why hadn't she told him? He had a right to know.

And anyway, she needed him with her at a time like this. Yet she'd been too damn pig-headed to pick up the phone and ask him to come. She clearly didn't have the sense of an amoeba when it came to taking care of herself or their child.

Once he had made sure everything was okay he was going to give her a good talking-to on that score. And then he was never going to let her or their child out of his sight again.

CHAPTER NINETEEN

LOUISA walked down the steps of the antenatal unit at University College Hospital, the heels of her stilettos clicking on the pavement as she headed down the street. She gave a shaky breath, exhaustion settling over her like an impenetrable fog. She'd been up until dawn, playing all the possible scenarios of today's scan through her head, and now all she wanted to do was sleep for a week. She needed to text Mel with her news and cry off their coffee date. She felt too drained right now even to talk to Mel, which had to be a first.

She was rooting around in her bag to find her mobile phone when the shrill screech of burning rubber split the early afternoon hush. Her head whipped round to see a familiar black convertible shudder to a halt at the kerb. The very last man on earth she wanted to see levered himself out of the car. He looked tall and gorgeous and as domineering as ever as he stalked towards her. The harsh pain stabbing at her heart did nothing to dim the familiar hum of arousal. She stiffened, hating herself. When had she become such a glutton for punishment?

'Have you had the scan?' he asked, towering over her.

She locked her knees and pushed her chin up. 'What are you doing here?'

He took her arm. 'Are you okay? Is the baby okay?'

'Why do you care?' she snapped back. She tried to pull her arm away. She didn't want him to touch her, but she had so little strength left he had no trouble holding her.

'Just answer the question. What did the doctor say?'

'Everything's fine,' she hissed, resentment burning inside her. Why was he doing this?

His fingers relaxed on her arm and his breath whooshed out. 'Are you sure?'

His voice wavered, almost as if he were scared to ask the question.

'Yes, I'm sure,' she said, determined not to analyse his reaction. What he thought about the baby didn't matter any more. She couldn't let it matter. 'Now, go away.'

She tugged her arm out of his grasp. But she'd gone less than three steps before he shouted behind her. 'Come back here. I want to talk about this.'

'Well, I don't,' she said, tossing the words over her shoulder, and carried on walking. She had to get away from him. If she fell apart in front of him she'd never forgive herself.

She heard his footsteps pounding on the pavement and then he was blocking her path. His hands rested on his hips and he had a scowl on his face. 'Why the hell didn't you tell me about the scan? About the GP not finding a heart-beat?'

Her fingers trembled as she clung to the shoulder strap of her bag. Why was he asking these things now, when it was too late? Was this some new form of torture he'd devised to make her suffer? 'Why would I tell you? You don't want to be involved—remember?'

His scowl deepened. 'I never said that. The baby's my child too.'

She could hear the panic in his voice, see the concern in his eyes, and had to steel herself not to be moved by it. This was just a knee-jerk reaction on his part. He felt guilty because of that sharp sense of responsibility of his. But duty wasn't enough—it wasn't love. She didn't need his protection or his charity, and neither did her child.

'It's not your child. Not any more,' she said. 'It's mine and I can cope without you. So you can stop worrying about us now.'

Luke was so stunned by the blank look on Louisa's face and the weary acceptance in her eyes that he couldn't speak. His huge relief that the baby was all right was replaced by a strangling sense of fear and loss which seemed to come from nowhere. Where was the fighting spirit that he'd always admired so much? Why did she look so drained? So sad?

She walked past him, but he pulled her round to face him.

'Of course you need me. How are you going to cope in that tiny flat? The child will be a bastard—and believe me that's no picnic,' he blurted out. She flinched at the ugly word and he softened his voice. 'And babies cost money—lots of money. Have you thought of that?' He stroked her arm, felt the slight shiver of response and thanked God for it. 'You look shattered, Louisa. You need me. The baby needs me.'

'Let go of my arm, Luke,' she murmured. He could see the dark smudges under her eyes and shame engulfed him. He did as she asked, feeling like the worst kind of bully.

'I needed you last night,' she said. 'While I was awake and panicking about what would happen today, what the doctor might find.'

'Why didn't you call me?' he said.

'I thought the baby was dead,' she said, as if he hadn't

spoken. The pain in her eyes was so vivid his shame turned to something black and ugly. 'I needed you to hold my hand, to tell me I was being an idiot, to tell me I was over-reacting. But you weren't there—because you chose not to be. And now it's too late.'

She turned to leave and desperation seized him. She wasn't going to walk away from him. Not again. He wouldn't let her. 'It's not too late. You said you loved me.' He threw the words at her like a drowning man in a stormy sea. 'If you really did you'd give us another chance.'

'A chance for what?' she said, the temper in her brown eyes making them flare to life at last. 'A chance for a casual affair that would fizzle out before the baby's even born? I won't settle for that. Not for me or my child.'

'We can live together,' he said. 'If that's what you want.'

Instead of accepting his olive branch, she snapped it off at the root.

'I don't want the grudging offer of a place to stay,' she said. 'I told you I loved you and you threw that back in my face. I wanted you to share this child, to be a real father to it, but you don't want that either. There's nothing to take a chance on. Can't you see that?'

The pity shadowing her eyes triggered a grinding feeling of inadequacy he thought he'd conquered a lifetime ago.

'You don't understand.' His voice broke on the words. 'It's not that I don't want to love you. It's not that I don't want to be a father to this child. It's that I can't—' He stopped. The something that had twisted inside him cracked open, leaving the same gaping chasm of despair and longing that he remembered from his childhood. 'It's that I can't love you.'

Louisa stared, shocked by the naked pain in his voice, the hopelessness in his eyes. Did he really believe that? But as his eyes flicked away from her face, the smoky grey pale with regret, she knew he did believe it.

The miserable depression that had seized her ever since she left Havensmere, that had made her cry herself to sleep every night thinking about all she'd lost—all she'd never really had—began to clear. A tiny flame of hope flickered to life in her chest. Was it possible that she'd been wrong about him all along? That he'd controlled his feelings and tried to control her in a misguided attempt to protect her?

'Why can't you love us?'

He thrust his hands into his pockets, hunching his shoulders. 'It doesn't matter,' he said.

'Of course it matters.' She could hear the pleading in her voice, and might have been ashamed of it. But her pride didn't seem to matter any more. Not when so much was at stake. 'Does this have something to do with your father?'

His head jerked up, and she saw the flash of vulnerability before he could control it.

Her instincts were correct. She'd known his father's rejection had hurt him, but why had it scarred him so deeply?

'I can't talk about this,' he said. 'We're in a public street and it's personal. And anyway, it's not remotely relevant.'

Louisa steeled herself against the anguish in his voice. She had to force this out into the open if she was ever going to get to the truth. 'We're only a short drive from the park. We'll have some privacy there.'

He seemed reluctant to agree, but nodded.

The drive took less than five minutes. As they drove into the outer circle Louisa was reminded of their first night together. The sweet romantic promise of the fresh spring breeze, the glittering twilight and those dewy pink blossoms. The grass was brown in patches now, after too many days without rain, and the air was sluggish and heavy after

a long hot city summer. The leaves on the trees were
already dying, the bright flowers beginning to shrivel up
and shed their blooms so they could go back into the earth
to survive the winter.

The evidence of nature's cycle made her smile, and she
let hope blossom inside her.

She'd done everything backwards where Luke was concerned. She'd conceived his child, then fallen in love with
him—and all before she'd ever really known him or understood him. He'd held himself back and tried to control the
uncontrollable, while she'd rushed headfirst into love
without taking the time to see why he was so scared to let
himself follow. Thanks to her own insecurities she'd
assumed he'd wanted to control her—when what he'd
really been doing was trying to control himself, to control
his feelings.

Once they were seated on a bench under an old maple
tree Louisa could see that Luke had been careful to hide
his unhappiness, his vulnerability. She wasn't about to let
him withdraw, though. Not this time.

'What happened with your father, Luke? What did he
do to you?'

He studied her. 'You're not going to let this go, are
you?'

'No, I'm not.' This was way too important.

He took a deep breath, turning away to stare at the grass
that edged the path. 'I asked him if I was really his son,'
he said thinly, 'and he slapped me across the face.'

Louisa gasped, covering her mouth with her hand. *Oh,
no.*

Luke didn't look round, so absorbed in the painful
memory she wasn't even sure he'd heard her. 'He told me
I was nothing more to him than an inconvenience, and if

I ever told anyone I was his son he'd cut me off without a penny and let me fend for myself.'

'Oh, Luke,' she whispered. 'How could anyone do that to a child? To a lonely, grieving child who was thousands of miles from home?'

He shrugged, the stiff jerk of his shoulder doing nothing to hide the pain. 'He changed his tune as he got older and realised he was never going to father another child. But by then I didn't need his money.'

'That's why you didn't want to acknowledge your relationship with him—because he had never acknowledged you.'

He turned to look at her and nodded, but his eyes had gone carefully blank. 'I despised him. I still do. But none of this has anything to do with our relationship—'

'He hurt you, Luke,' she interrupted softly. She laid her hand on his arm and felt the tremble of emotion he couldn't disguise. 'He made you think you didn't matter. Don't you see you're letting him win by closing yourself off? By convincing yourself that you can't love anyone, that you don't deserve it? You had to do that when you were a child. You don't have to do it any more. I offered you my love. Why won't you take it?'

'Damn it.' He leant forward and sunk his head in his hands. 'I can't take it.' The words were muffled but she could still hear the misery in them.

She bent close to him, stroked his thigh, felt the iron-hard muscles tight with tension. 'Why can't you take it?'

'Because it wouldn't be fair.' He ran his hands through his hair, gave a deep sigh. His eyes met hers, the look in them sharp and wary. 'You're such a romantic, Louisa. You think you can love me and it'll all be okay. But it won't be. I'll make a terrible father. I've always known that.

I wanted to support the baby, to give it all the things I never had. But I won't be able to love it any more than I'll be able to love you. I don't seem to be able to get close to anyone. Something died inside me that day. And I killed it. Not him.'

Tears clogged her throat as she listened to the pain in his voice, saw the torment in his eyes. He'd spent so much of his life learning how *not* to need anyone. Now that he did he had no idea what to do. She swallowed the tears down and took his cheeks in her palms, kissed him full on the mouth.

'Shut up, Luke,' she said, giving his head an impatient shake. She stroked his cheeks, felt the fine rasp of his stubble. 'You didn't kill anything—and neither did he, even though he tried. You're not going to make a terrible father. You're going to make a wonderful one. And you're going to make a wonderful husband too—when you get over this silly notion you have about love being some big, scary thing you're not allowed to have.'

'You can't know that,' he said, his voice quiet and forlorn.

She grasped his hand and stood up, tugging him off the bench. 'You want to know what I see when I look at you?'

'I'm not sure I want to hear this,' he said.

She wrapped her arms around his waist, gazed up at that harsh, handsome face. 'I see a man who believed he couldn't be a father yet felt fiercely protective towards his child. A man who cooked for me, cared for me, and worried about me even though he barely knew me. I see a man who's made a home out of a place he thought he hated. A man who always puts my pleasure before his own, and a man who can make me laugh even when he's driving me nuts. But most of all I see a man who needs me as much as I need him.'

She slid her hands up his back, held him close as she buried her head in his chest. She felt the heavy weight of his hands on her shoulders, saw the uncertainty in his eyes as she looked up. And she loved him even more.

He cupped her cheek, rubbed it as she leant into his palm. 'You're scaring me to death, Louisa. You know that, right?'

'I know it's a leap of faith, and you're not used to those. But you can't hide for the rest of your life.' She sent him a watery smile. 'You've needed a home for a long time. And our baby needs one too. We can make one together at Havensmere, or in London, or wherever we want. But it'll be so much stronger and better than anything we could make apart.'

'Are you sure you want to risk it?' he said, sounding amazed. 'I'm warning you, I don't even know where to start.'

'You've started already,' she said, grinning. 'You just haven't been paying attention.'

He held her head in his hands, lowered his mouth to hers and murmured, 'Okay, you're on. But I'm warning you. Now I've got you I'm never letting you go.'

'Same goes for me,' she whispered back, and her heart overflowed.

As Luke's lips covered hers, he felt the same emotional upheaval that had scared him from the first moment he'd met her. But this time the insistent need to draw back—to protect himself, to protect her—didn't come. His fingers dug into the firm flesh of her buttocks as his tongue tangled with hers, and he heard the soft purr deep in her throat that signalled her arousal.

This time he let himself fall—and felt the pure unfettered rush of excitement, joy and exhilaration.

After so many years alone he'd finally found home.

EPILOGUE

'I THINK I hate you—how come you look so fabulous already?' Mel grumbled, pushing her sunglasses down and giving Louisa's bikini-clad figure a pointed once-over.

Louisa put her glass of lemonade on the poolside table and gave her friend a deliberately smug smile. 'Secrets of the rich and famous, honey,' she said, tapping her nose. 'We don't share them with mere mortals, you know.'

'Good grief,' Mel scoffed. 'I knew this whole Lady Berwick thing would go straight to your head.'

Louisa laughed at Mel's comically sour expression. They both knew Louisa's figure was nowhere near as trim as it had been a year ago.

Six months after an excruciating thirteen-hour labour— during which she'd called her new husband every name under the sun—Louisa's boobs were still enormous, and even though little Viscount Berwick seemed happy to breastfeed twenty-four-seven, she couldn't seem to lose the extra stone she'd been carrying around in post-pregnancy love handles ever since his birth. She knew she would never regain the lean, perfectly toned figure she'd once taken for granted. And she couldn't have cared less about it. After all, she'd never been happier in her life—and anyway, her husband had demonstrated only this morning how much he adored her new 'Mother Earth' look.

Louisa leaned back on her sun lounger, her cheeks glowing as she thought of just what she and Luke had got up to that morning, while their son had had one of his rare lie-ins. She gazed at the two most important people in her life. The smile that was never far away crept back across her face.

Standing on the pool terrace, where he'd once given her the most unromantic marriage proposal known to man, Luke looked deliciously rumpled in a pair of damp swimming trunks and the garish 'Elvis in Hawaii' shirt she'd got him for Christmas. His dark hair—which he kept threatening to get cut—flowed in wavy strands to his collar and dripped on the chartreuse silk of the shirt. He'd forgotten to shave after all the excitement of their elicit tryst in the shower that morning. The stubble shadowing his jaw would have made him look more like a pirate than a lord of the realm if it hadn't been for the baby cuddled against his chest.

Little Luca Alfredo Devereaux was in his favourite place in all the world: snuggled in the crook of his daddy's arm, one small fist stuffed in his cupid's bow mouth and the other gripping his daddy's hair. After twenty minutes of playing in the pool with his father, and Mel's three children, her baby boy was utterly exhausted, but his eyelids kept blinking open as he gazed owlishly up at his father.

Standing next to Louisa's two main men was Mel's husband Jack, whose ten-month-old daughter Clare was already fast asleep on his shoulder. With Cal and Ella playing in the sandpit which Luke and Jack had put together that morning, it was the first moment of calm they'd had since the Devlin brood had arrived for the long

August weekend three hours ago, and she and Mel were making the most of it.

There was nothing Louisa DiMarco Devereaux would rather do than gaze lovingly at her men. As she watched, she saw Luke put his large hand on his son's back and pat, rocking the baby instinctively while he continued his conversation with Jack. After a few seconds their son's head drooped onto Luke's shoulder, his fist released its death grip on his father's hair, and his compact little body softened against the hard muscles of his father's chest. The sunbeam inside Louisa shimmered, making her feel as if she were lit from within. How could that man ever have believed he wouldn't be a good father?

She sighed, tears welling in her eyes.

'There's just something about men and babies that gets me every time,' Mel murmured beside her.

Louisa glanced round to see Mel's eyes as suspiciously bright as her own as she stared across the pool at her own husband.

Louisa sniffed and huffed out a laugh, wiping the tear of joy from her cheek. 'Look at us—if those two catch us blubbing like this we'll never hear the end of it.'

Mel grinned back and gave her own cheeks a quick swipe. 'Don't worry, they're far too busy boring themselves to death talking about football, or some other twaddle.'

Louisa smiled and closed her eyes, all the sleep she'd lost the night before beginning to claim her. 'Goodness, Mel—how did we get to be so lucky?'

'It's not luck, Lou. We had to work really hard to get those guys up to scratch—and we've both got the frown lines and the stretch marks to prove it.'

'I suppose,' Louisa murmured sleepily, a contented grin

on her face. 'But it's worth every single solitary one of them, isn't it?'

She took a deep breath as her eyelids fluttered down, and tasted the heady scent of Havensmere's flowers which Luke and she had planted together that spring.

As she drifted off to sleep she contemplated the argument she and Luke were going to have when she told him she'd forgotten to take her contraceptive pill that morning. And the fantastic make-up sex they would be having soon after.

And then she pictured all the other little Devereauxes they were going to make together in the years to come. In the midst of the warm, fuzzy dream, another little frown line formed on her brow. She better make sure some of them were girls. After all, she didn't want to be totally outnumbered…

HARLEQUIN *Presents*

International Billionaires

Life is a game of power and pleasure.
And these men play to win!

THE FRENCH TYCOON'S PREGNANT MISTRESS
by Abby Green

As mistress to French tycoon Pascal Lévêque,
innocent Alana learns just how much pleasure can
be had in the bedroom. But now she's pregnant,
and Pascal vows he'll take her up the aisle!

Book #2814

Available April 2009

Eight volumes in all to collect!

Sicilian by name...scandalous,
scorching and seductive by nature!

CAPTIVE AT THE SICILIAN BILLIONAIRE'S COMMAND
by *Penny Jordan*

Three darkly handsome Leopardi men must hunt down
their missing heir. It is their duty—as Sicilians, as sons,
as brothers! The scandal and seduction they will leave in
their wake is just the beginning....

Book #2811

Available April 2009

**Look out for the next two stories in this
fabulous new trilogy from Penny Jordan:**

**THE SICILIAN BOSS'S MISTRESS in May
THE SICILIAN'S BABY BARGAIN in August**

www.eHarlequin.com

HP12811

kept for his *Pleasure*

She's his mistress on demand!

THE SECRET MISTRESS ARRANGEMENT
by *Kimberly Lang*

When tycoon Matt Jacobs meets Ella MacKenzie, he throws away the rule book and spends a week in bed! And after seven days of Matt's lovemaking, Ella's accepting a very indecent proposal....

Book #2818

Available April 2009

Don't miss any books in this exciting new miniseries from Harlequin Presents!

REQUEST YOUR FREE BOOKS!

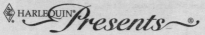

2 FREE NOVELS PLUS 2 FREE GIFTS!

YES! Please send me 2 FREE Harlequin Presents® novels and my 2 FREE gifts (gifts are worth about $10). After receiving them, if I don't wish to receive any more books, I can return the shipping statement marked "cancel". If I don't cancel, I will receive 6 brand-new novels every month and be billed just $4.05 per book in the U.S. or $4.74 per book in Canada, plus 25¢ shipping and handling per book and applicable taxes, if any*. That's a savings of close to 15% off the cover price! I understand that accepting the 2 free books and gifts places me under no obligation to buy anything. I can always return a shipment and cancel at any time. Even if I never buy another book, the two free books and gifts are mine to keep forever.

106 HDN ERRW   306 HDN ERRL

Name _____ (PLEASE PRINT)

Address _____ Apt. # _____

City _____ State/Prov. _____ Zip/Postal Code _____

Signature (if under 18, a parent or guardian must sign)

Mail to the Harlequin Reader Service:
IN U.S.A.: P.O. Box 1867, Buffalo, NY 14240-1867
IN CANADA: P.O. Box 609, Fort Erie, Ontario L2A 5X3

Not valid to current subscribers of Harlequin Presents books.

**Want to try two free books from another line?
Call 1-800-873-8635 or visit www.morefreebooks.com.**

* Terms and prices subject to change without notice. N.Y. residents add applicable sales tax. Canadian residents will be charged applicable provincial taxes and GST. Offer not valid in Quebec. This offer is limited to one order per household. All orders subject to approval. Credit or debit balances in a customer's account(s) may be offset by any other outstanding balance owed by or to the customer. Please allow 4 to 6 weeks for delivery. Offer available while quantities last.

Your Privacy: Harlequin Books is committed to protecting your privacy. Our Privacy Policy is available online at www.eHarlequin.com or upon request from the Reader Service. From time to time we make our lists of customers available to reputable third parties who may have a product or service of interest to you. If you would prefer we not share your name and address, please check here. ☐

HP08R

UNEXPECTED BABIES

One night, one pregnancy!

These four men may be from all over the world–
Italy, a Desert Kingdom, Britain and Argentina–
but there's one thing they all have in common....

When their mistresses fall pregnant after
one passionate night, an illegitimate heir is
unthinkable. The mothers-to-be will become
convenient wives!

Look for all of the fabulous stories available in April:

Androletti's Mistress #49
by MELANIE MILBURNE

The Desert King's Pregnant Bride #50
by ANNIE WEST

The Pregnancy Secret #51
by MAGGIE COX

The Vásquez Mistress #52
by SARAH MORGAN

www.eHarlequin.com

HPE0409

You're invited to join our Tell Harlequin Reader Panel!

By joining our new reader panel you will:

- Receive Harlequin® books—they are FREE and yours to keep with no obligation to purchase anything!
- Participate in fun online surveys
- Exchange opinions and ideas with women just like you
- Have a say in our new book ideas and help us publish the best in women's fiction

In addition, you will have a chance to win great prizes and receive special gifts!
See Web site for details. Some conditions apply.
Space is limited.

To join, visit us at

www.TellHarlequin.com.